William Bradford, William Brotherhead

Forty years among the old booksellers of Philadelphia, with bibliographical remarks

William Bradford, William Brotherhead

Forty years among the old booksellers of Philadelphia, with bibliographical remarks

ISBN/EAN: 9783337115272

Printed in Europe, USA, Canada, Australia, Japan

Cover: Foto ©Andreas Hilbeck / pixelio.de

More available books at **www.hansebooks.com**

FORTY YEARS

AMONG THE

OLD BOOKSELLERS

OF

PHILADELPHIA,

WITH

BIBLIOGRAPHICAL REMARKS.

BY

W. BROTHERHEAD,

AUTHOR OF THE CENTENNIAL BOOK OF THE SIGNERS OF THE DECLARATION
OF INDEPENDENCE, ETC., ETC.

A. P. BROTHERHEAD,
1440 SOUTH STREET, PHILADELPHIA.
1891.

FORTY YEARS

AMONG THE

OLD BOOKSELLERS

IN

PHILADELPHIA.

By W. BROTHERHEAD,
OLD BOOKSELLER.

I HAVE been solicited by many old friends to relate my experience as an old bookseller for the last forty years. I have succumbed to their desires, and in doing so I have resolved to make a plain statement.

The position of old bookseller is so totally different from any other trade that it requires special mention and fuller explanation. A grocer sells his candles, a tailor fits his customer, a dry goods man sells his goods; each article has its special merits, which are duly

(3)

described by its seller, then the matter is ended. The qualifications required in each of the above depart-ments are of a general mediocre character, such as any one with ordinary brains can soon learn—a few months are generally sufficient. The old bookseller—one who is worthy of the name—must have high qualifications, besides the mere *objective* merits of the general trades-men. The first requisite he requires is a thorough knowledge of literature—he should be a cyclopædia, able to answer questions about the general nature of books, and their authors. The whole field of history he should know, from Homer to Macaulay. The new discoveries in history, either biblical or general, he should know. The latest discoveries in Egyptian history, such as the 3000 years old papyri, with the biblical discoveries of Tischendorf and other profound scholars—all should be known by him. I do not mean a very *profound* knowledge, but a *general* one.

I am aware that in the *past*, as well as the *present*, mere old ragmen—old junk dealers—have been and are metamorphosed into old booksellers—a disgrace to its high intellectual worth. I am also aware of some who are mere *catalogue old booksellers*, and who, par-rot-like, can spin you off the latest books collected by a Bohn or Quaritch, but are not aware of the con-tents of any of the books, nor of the special idiosyn-cracies of the authors. Such booksellers I would recommend to read all of Dibdin's works, published under the patronage of the Earl of Spencer; "Censuria Literati;" "Lowndc's Bibliographers' Manual," edited by H. Bohn; Brunet's "Manual of Bibliography;" Watt's great work on Bibliography; Rich's "American Bibliography;" Stevens' "Nuggets." These works will furnish them with the *basis* of bibliography —a knowledge of books—on which they can build by *experience* a superstructure that will honor their profession. Goldsmith, in his "Vicar of Wakefield," talks about "Shakespeare and the musical glasses;" how few of our booksellers can do this! Charles Lamb, the kindly and most interesting of litterateurs, should be read and studied. Hazlitt, in his brilliant criticisms, and Leigh Hunt, in his Essays, are worthy of careful perusal.

These are a few hints thrown out for the especial attention of old booksellers, but only a few; the whole scope of general literature should be scanned over, and in process of time the brain would be so filled with special literature that it would be a feast for the gods.

In 1849 I commenced to sell old books at the north west corner of Sixth and Market streets. My stock was worth about $60. It did not fill up my shelves, and I added cigars to my stock, and filled the empty shelves with cigar-boxes. These in a short time I took down, and in their place I covered the empty shelves with Catlin's portraits of Indians. These being highly colored, made a good show. "Annuals" were the fashion at this day—as fashionable as a lady's bonnet is now; no one could do without the "Snow-lake," "Iris," and many others.

I bought my books chiefly at auction—then carried on by G. W. Lord, at the southeast corner of Sixth and Decatur streets.

The old book trade was essentially different to what it is now. American books were not so plentiful, and the English sales chiefly supplied our wants.

Lumley of London sent over large invoices of miscellaneous books, most of them the trash of the London auction houses. I have seen him buy thousands of volumes at auction for the American market. Willis and Southeran were large exporters to this city; their books were of a good quality, many of them were large folios and quartos illustrated with colored plates, engraved on copper and in aqua tint. This class of books are not even common in the London market, and are catalogued at prices 50 per cent. higher than they were bought forty years ago.

Dramatic books were common. Mrs. Inchbald, Cumberland and Bells Editions, were a drug on the market and brought at auction from 10 to 15 cents per volume. They would bring twice the price to-day at auction. Dramatic memoirs were also in plenty. Tate Wilkinson's Memoirs in 4 volumes; The Itinerant in 4 volumes, Life of Garrick, Mrs. Siddons, Edmund Kean, The Kembles, Cooke and others, I imported and sold for about 50 cents per volume. In the London market to-day these books sell at one dollar per volume and upwards.

Americana, or books on America, were not much in request forty years ago. About 1850 I commenced importing English books, those that were curious and rare, among them many curious books on America. I know of but three men in this city at that time that bought them; those were E. D. Ingraham, Jabez Fisher, R. C. Davis and John McAllister, now dead, was one of my earliest customers; nearly every morning he came with green bag and often bought of me. His fine library, rich in local history, is now in possession of his son William, who appreciates it highly; all the family are lovers of books. Ingraham and Davis are dead; of Fisher I am not sure whether alive or not. I have sketched the character of Ingraham in my memoir of him in the "Lives of Eminent Philadelphians," which I published in 1859. I will only add here, that he was one of the most original bibliopoles I have ever met. He was eccentric in person, witty in his sayings, a dry humor prevaded his conversation—it had the bou-

quet of Dibdin, and was highly flavored with anec-
dotes of the most distinguished men in Europe. I
recollect on one occasion, and the only one, I had a
copy of a very rare book then, and extremely rare
now, "The Memoirs of Harriett Wilson, a Woman
of Pleasure." Mr. Ingraham had a copy of it which
was illustrated with portraits, autographs and newspaper cuttings. Harriett Wilson gave the names of
many of her patrons; among them was the Duke of
Wellington. In order to confirm this statement, he
wrote to a special friend of his in London, and he
found out that the statement was true, and included
many other highly distinguished persons. About
this time I added to my importation of old books,
old engravings and *autographs*. Ingraham spent many
a day in looking over my collection, and added many
rare historical prints with which his famous collection of books was illustrated. The collection of R. C.
Davis' books and autographs was chiefly indebted to
my importations; so was Fisher's, Dr. Koecker's, F. J.
Dreer's famous collection of autographs, which he
has generously given to the Pennsylvania Historical
Society of this city. In 1857 I published in my
"American Notes and Queries," a full description of this
collection. This description was afterwards printed
in *quarto form* on *card paper;* twenty-five copies were
only printed and given away.

After importing for four years, I found the mania for collecting books on America was gradually increasing. I instructed my agent to collect everything in America he could find, either in books, engravings or autographs.

The Americana fever increased very rapidly. Ingraham died; his collection of books was sold at auction, comprising over 17,000 volumes. Every nook and corner of his house was packed with books—many were found that were claimed by different persons. His penchant was first to buy—if the persons would not sell he would borrow, and rarely return—the book he must have at any cost, even at the risk of honor—at least a pardonable sin. This gave the great impetus for buying American books, or *old books* on America, illustrated with every device imaginable. The mania gradually pervaded every city —east, west, north and south. New York at this time, from 1852 and in that decennial period, had not fairly started. She had not any special booksellers for many years that supplied the wants of a few collectors who were ardent in their desires to augment their collections. Mr. Menzies, a Scotchman, had risen from the ranks of labor, and became a wealthy man —a kind and generous one, without bluster—modest in all his dealings, and exhibited a rare taste in the selections of books he desired. He not only bought

the most *recherche* editions, but they were almost im-
maculate in condition. *Uncut* copies were his chief
aim, and for them he would pay a generous price.
At the time when Irving was urged by his literary
publisher, Mr. Putnam, to write a " Life of Washington," he was influenced to do this by men like Menzies—the result was a Life of Washington by Irving.
Its appearance caught at the flood-tide of Americana,
and the rage for illustration of books was at its height.
Irving's Washington was the chief book, and on it
Mr. Menzies lavished his money in profusion. At
that time I was the chief importer of books in
America, including old engravings and autographs;
and for the purpose of illustrating this book, Messrs.
Menzies, Bailey, Myers, John Munroe, John Allen,
and other New York collectors, made me many visits,
and bought liberally.

Mr. Menzies found age and debility creeping on
him, and not having any one in his own family
that appreciated his efforts, he wisely concluded to
sell his famous, and in many respects unique, collection of books. The library was sold at auction; the
catalogue was got up in superb style—a fitting ac-
companiment to his unrivaled collection of books.
The prices the books brought were complimentary to
their owner; yet, I presume, they did not bring the
original cost. Irving's " Life of Washington" was

his *chef d'œuvre*. It was illustrated, with several original letters of Washington, original water colors of
scenes depicted in the Life, rare views and portraits;
bound in 7 volumes, quarto, and bought by Joseph
Drexel for $7,000. How much more pleasant it was
for Mr. Menzies to ponder and reflect on the acts of
his past life, that his princely expenditures on books
aggregated for his family an income that would keep
them living a luxurious life! How many princely
incomes have been spent on horses, yachting-club life,
and countless debaucheries and gambling generally,
ending in bankruptcy, suicide, or in poverty! Such
business as book collecting, and other kindred subjects, are near akin to genius, and whose names live
in history, while the others mentioned are pointed to
as cases of demoralization, and always subject to censure—in fact, are black spots always to be avoided.

In January, 1857, I commenced the issue of
"*American Notes and Queries;*" this was the *first*
American magazine devoted to this subject matter.
It was succeeded a few months later by the " *Histori-*
cal Magazine," published in New York. I only
issued four numbers, my means being too limited for
any further delivery ; 500 copies were issued, and it is
now very *scarce*, and when sold at auction, brings
generally more than its original price, which is not a
common thing in magazines. At this time a well-

known name in this city, and a peculiar personality, was a frequent visitor at my store, then 213 S. 8th street—Charles A. Poulson. He was a tall, erect man, somewhat pompous in his manner, and reticent to all but his friends. His penchant was the collection of *local views* of this city; many he painted in water colors from memory. His home on Front street, one of the old aristocratic residences 100 years ago, and I presume built by his celebrated father, the originator, editor and printer of the *North American*, was literally covered with local views. I am indebted to him for several historical views published in my first " *Book of the Signers of the Declaration of Independence.*" I wished to have a view of the house in which Washington lived, in Market street below Sixth street, south side, now part of Wanamaker's store, southeast corner of Sixth and Market streets. On making careful inquiry, I found none had been made. I then inquired of my old friend John McAllister, an old respected Philadelphian. He knew of none, but referred me to our mutual friend C. A. Poulson. I saw him: he had none. I then knew of his local sketches, and asked him if he could not draw one from memory. He said he would try. He did so. When finished I then showed it to Mr. McAllister and other old residents, and all pronounced it good. He also drew from memory the *views* in my " *Book of the Signers,*"

" *Fort Wilson*," and "*Thomas McKean's House*," these were all pronounced correct by men who had seen them. Mr. Poulson died soon after he made these views for me; and let us ever remember that the antique collection of scrap-books filled with illustrations and newspaper cuttings, were given by him and are now in the Philadelphia Library, of the greatest value to local history. I feel great pleasure in noting here that John A. McAllister, Jr., requested Mr. Poulson to give his collection to the Library, and that John A. McAllister paid the whole expense of mounting them. Such men are rare, and let us pay homage to those who devote their time and money to such researches.

In 1850 we had about 300,000 in population; but a greater ratio of old book collectors were active then than now with a population estimated over 1,000,000. In the 50's we had fifteen old booksellers. In 1890, with a population three times as great, not more than twelve can be counted worth mentioning. This state of things, in a literary sense, is truly degrading to us as an intelligent and cultured city; and, however we may boast of our increased manufactures and general increase of business, we are sadly wanting in all the elements which distinguish Paris, London, Berlin, Vienna, or Rome; in a word, our life is more objective than subjective—is more animal than intel-

lectual. We had far more old book collectors, far
more collectors of old engravings and autographs,
with 300,000, than we now have with over 1,000,000
of people. Wealth and learning have always in Europe gone hand in hand together; but our desires and
highest ambition trend to the grossly material part of
our nature. I must not omit to notice the princely
sums of money that have been given by Dr. Rush, of
this city, Peabody, Astor, Pratt, Carnegie, and others,
to the erection of costly buildings and the furnishing
of costly books to the different libraries. These valuable gifts, at least, show that amid the turmoil and
activities of business the latent idea of an intellectual
life is not forgotten. All praise to these noble souls
for such acts.

In 1859 I conceived the idea of making a book
containing *fac simile* letters of each Signer of the
Declaration of Independence, and other matters pertaining to them. This I accomplished, and in 1860
published it. It may be pertinent to state here that
this book is the only *one* in the world that contains
a complete monument to the founders of the nation
and of our great Republic. England has its Magna
Charta, and *fac similes* can be had of it on an illuminated sheet, but the *seals* only of those men who
wrung from King John this immortal document are
only to be seen. I had a number of subscribers—

several from the South. Dr. Gibbes, a well-known
writer and historian, was a subscriber ; in 1860 when
the late Rebellion was in its first throes, when South
Carolina became hotly belligerent, when she first or-
ganized her rebellious forces, when everything was
red hot, Dr. Gibbes paid a last visit to his old friend
Dr. Samuel Jackson. He paid me a visit, and paid for
his copy, adding that "it would be the last money he
would pay me as a citizen of the United States." Alas
for him and his associates, it did not prove to be true.
As a mark of his worth the Rebel Government made
him Surgeon in Chief of the Confederate Army. He
is now dead, and peace to his ashes. Another singular circumstance of the late war occurred: One of my
subscribers from Norfolk, Virginia, a well-known book
collector, a minister of the Protestant Episcopal
Church, whose name I now forget, desired me to send
his copy by express, and C. O. D. on delivery. This
was done, and the money sent by express—it was all
in *five-cent pieces*— with a note stating he was sorry
to send such small money, but war was afloat everywhere, and Virginia would soon be out of the Union.

As a mark of respect to Queen Victoria, I had a
folio copy of my book sent to her through the United
States Minister at the Court of St. James, G. M.
Dallas, formerly Vice-President of the United States,
and of this city. When the courtly and highly-

talented Minister returned to this city from England, he one morning brought me a letter of thanks from Lord John Russell, who was then Home Secretary. I shall never forget that fine manly presence with his beauty and gray hair, and how courtly he flattered me in presenting such a fine copy to the Queen of England. This copy I had bound in full Levant Turkey morocco. The sides were emblazoned with the coat of arms of both countries. The sides of the book were covered with the finest leather, and cut in diamond shape, and in each diamond was the eagle and the lion in each alternate diamond.

In 1861 the war was fairly commenced, business was paralyzed, war, war, was the cry everywhere, all business except that of war was thrown aside, old book collectors locked up their libraries, then engravings and autographs were thrown aside and men buckled on their war armor, and on they went to Washington to fight for their country. Newspaper literature took the place of books. No one had any time to read except war news, and amid all this excitement for one year books were forgotten. When the movements of the various armies began, exciting episodes almost daily occurred, the chief and earliest among them was the movements of General Fremont in the southwest, especially that masterly retreat of General Sigel when General Price attacked him with.

superior numbers. General Fremont's policy was somewhat novel and drastic in its character, and his enemies showed him no mercy. It was to his rescue from such undeserved censure that I wrote in his defense one of the first pamphlets of war literature entitled "General Fremont and the injustice done him by politicians and envious military men." In 1862 war literature was fairly commenced and all other literature was subordinated to it. It may be truly stated that the history of the world cannot show a war literature to equal either in quantity or quality, that which we possess.

In 1860 I commenced my Circulating Library at 218 South Eighth Street. From the large stock of old books which I had, I selected the nucleus of my library, and added to it the *new* books as they were issued. I still continued buying and selling old books, while the patrons to my library daily increased. The success of my library caused me to pay more attention to it than old-book selling, and this business of the library was my chief care. The lease of my store, 218 South Eighth Street, ended in 1863, and at that time, when the war absorbed every person and every action, I found it difficult to rent a suitable place. I however rented 911 Locust Street, and added such alterations as I deemed necessary.

In 1867, I bought the property No. 205 South Thir-

2

teenth Street. I pulled the old building down and erected a new house, and made the first story for my library, and to it I moved in November, 1867. I still continued old-book buying and selling, and used the basement of my house for that purpose. At this time I had 50,000 volumes in my library, and I can say, without egotism, that in number of volumes and first-class literature it had not its equal in the United States as a circulating library.

I *imported* many of the *new English* books as were issued which were not *republished* in this country, and added to them American books. This was the *distinctive* character of my library, and as such it was patronized by the *élite* of this city and its suburbs. I was proud of my library and especially of my patrons, and felt gratified by my success.

In addition to my library in this city, I was solicited to open one in Pottsville, Wilkesbarre, Washington, D. C., Elkton, Md., and Dover, Del. These were all in existence for some time, until the persons with whom I had made arrangements either died or changed their business. This method of diffusing knowledge should meet with the approbation of all good people, and I as the main instrument in this method feel, I have at least rendered valuable assistance to obtain general knowledge.

About 1877 commenced the issue of cheap literature; the Lakeside Series was commenced in Chicago; the Seaside followed, with numerous other issues that affected all libraries like mine.

In 1878 I met with a serious accident by falling on the ice, and injured my spine. For several months I was seriously sick under Dr. John Brinton's care—at least he advised me to go to Europe, as my nervous condition was so shattered by the fall. This meant a relinquishment of my business, which to me was a sad loss; but as my health was paramount over all, I sold out my business, first at private sale, and afterwards at auction. I spent most of 1878 and 1879 in England, and felt somewhat better, but it took me five years before I fully recovered my health.

This statement breaks my chronological arrangement, and I must now refer back to 1875. The Centennial was the talk of the day; everything was in active preparation for the next year, 1876. Such a great event as the celebration of the *first century* of our Republic I thought should be honored in a fitting manner with a special literary monument to its founders. I resolved to issue a *second* series of my "*Book of the Signers.*" This second series is *additional* to the matter in my first book. The *fac-simile letters* are a *new issue*, the historical matter *new* and more complete. I made an arrangement with Joseph M. Stoddard for its publication—I furnishing all the material printed on sheets, and he binding the book or issuing it in numbers as he thought fit. I added many *original illustrations* to this edition which at the time I published my first series I could not obtain.

The issues of *new books* on this grand occasion were so numerous that I doubt if a dozen succeeded in making expenses. I lost in money, exclusive of labor and time, over $5,000. This harassed me pecuniarily so that I never fully recovered from it, and do not expect to. All this patriotic devotion and irksome labor elicited only plain, bald sympathy, but only a particle of material aid. I still live comfortably and humbly, and though I cannot boast of my thousands of dollars, yet my books will live as long as the Republic exists—nay, they can never die, while an historical scholar lives or our grand libraries exist. This is poor consolation in a money point of view; but the poor scholar looks to a brighter future, not tinged with the dross of gold.

After my return from England in 1879, I again got quietly into business with about 1,000 volumes of old books. I chiefly sold to booksellers in different parts of the country by catalogue and otherwise; but I yearned to again commence business in my old style, and my health being gradually restored, I opened my present book store, 1440 South street, with a very limited stock, and still live in a very humble manner; and though now in my 67th year, I still feel vigorous, and hope to die in harness.

Having given an account of my personal identity in old bookselling for over forty years, I propose to sketch a few of my co-laborers in the same business, thus partially filling up gaps of local history that some future local historian may use.

APLEY.

The Arcade in Chesnut street, between Sixth and Seventh streets, north side, was purchased some years ago by the late Dr. Jayne. This fine old building he pulled down, and erected in the place several fine stores which are used for wholesale purposes. The Arcade had many claims for admiration. Its architecture was somewhat novel and ornate. The front on Chesnut street had architectural beauties which the present stores cannot claim. There was a well-patronized restaurant and several stores fronting on Chesnut street. The entrance into Decatur street contained many small stores on each side. These stores resembled a bazaar by the motley appearance of the various goods offered for sale.

In one of those stores resided a very dirty man, surrounded on all sides by a collection of old books almost without form, scattered here and there without any classification. He was a man of about fifty years of age or thereabouts; he might have been older, but his dirty and ragged appearance made it difficult to say how old he was. He always looked dark and sallow. His features were not repulsive to look at, but they had that *miserly cast* which at one glance caused him to be a marked character. The windows of his store were so thick with dirt and rubbish that it was difficult to see the titles of the books. I have many times visited the store for the purpose of purchasing books, and in looking round through the vistas of shelves erected at random, you would see him in some nook or corner lift up his bedizened face, and if early in the morning he would be cooking or eating his breakfast. The smell of the room, with the mustiness of the old books and the smell of his eatables, was anything but savory or cleanly. The description which Dickens gives in "Old Curiosity Shop," of the store in which Little Nell's grandfather lived, is nothing to compare with old Apley's store in the Arcade. As far as my recollection carries me, he slept and lived in this dirty atmosphere of old books. If he was married, and I think he was not, I never in all my visits saw the appearance of a womanly face, or any signs of womanly care and attention. I think he was an American. My conversations with him were not numerous, but I have not the faintest idea that he possessed any bibliographical knowledge of books. He died in the fifties. I am not sure of the year, but his store for some time was carried on by one of his brothers, who soon relinquished it and went into another business.

DUROSS.

Duross is dead. He was a specimen of the rough, gruff Irishman; a rough diamond—though he had kindly impulses, and to those that knew him, he was a good fellow. His old book store was in the Arcade near to Apley's, and though his stock was not large, yet it was well selected. His business was very limited; he had some means which did not render it imperative that his daily bread depended on his profits from sales of books. Mr. Duross died at an advanced age.

JAMES DALLING.

Dalling was a Scotchman, of the old school. He kept a very select collection of old books for sale on South Eighth street, above Chestnut, east side, now Green's hotel, and was well patronized by book buy-ers. He was a man of more than ordinary education, and attracted the best class of book buyers. He was not a man who stooped to conquer, but was firm in all his dealings, and with all the canny characteristics of his race. He, like the majority of old booksellers,

did not amass a fortune; in fact, the pure and un-
adulterated old bookseller seldom does more than live
comfortably, collect stock, and feast among his books,
and love to talk to his literary customers of the great
geniuses in the Elizabethan age, and descant on the
talents and greatness of the age of Queen Anne.

JOHN PENNINGTON.

The Pennington family was of old Quaker stock, and
John Pennington added honor and probity to the old
family connections. He was a well educated man, and
courtly both in personality and conduct; in fact, he
was a gentleman of the old school. I have been informed he was a clerk in the Custom House. While
there he began to purchase books to suit his own
tastes, which were those of a *belle lettres* class. Some
reason occasioned him to leave his position, and he
took the books he had collected and opened an old
book store on South Fourth street, below Market,
west side. He was a good French scholar, and part
of his stock was French books. He commenced the
importation of old books, both French and English,
and this scholarly man soon attracted around him a
coterie of literary men learned in book lore and accomplished in manners.

Before the abolition of slavery in the South, when
their paternal governments were in full sway, when

fortunes were made out of the poor slaves, then flourished the literary Augustan age of the South. Let it be said to the credit of these men that they cultivated the hereditary literary instincts of their Anglo-Saxon forefathers. The money made from the work of these slaves was haughtily and grandly spent in educating their children in the best schools of Europe. The sons were trained for the various professions, and the most accomplished teachers that Europe could furnish were employed for their higher education. The results were that in proportion to their population, the Southerners produced a class of men, both in numbers and general culture, that far exceeded those in the Middle and Eastern States. The history of the country shows that, up to 1860, when the Rebellion broke out in its greatest ferocity, the South, in both the Congress and the Senate, shows a greater galaxy of brilliant men than all the rest of the States combined. However censurable and questionable this mode of government may be considered by many, it cannot be denied that it produced a class of men always to be admired by the literary student, that we in the North have as yet failed to produce.

It was this class of men who were the chief patrons of John Pennington. Most of these men were excellent French scholars, and they required French books. John Pennington had commenced the importation of these books, and for many years he had the chief business in his hands. The New York booksellers, forty years ago, had scarcely thought of this line of business.

Mr. Christern, a German, opened a book store under the National Theatre, then leased by W. E. Burton, and which was burned down, and in its place now stands the Continental hotel. In one of the stores attached to the theatre, on Chestnut street, Mr. Christern sold foreign books and engravings. He did not occupy the store long, but took his business to New York, and there finally commenced the sale of foreign books, and I think still continues.

Mr. Pennington's store become the centre of the *elite litterateurs* of this city, and of men like Charles Sumner and others. When the literary men of the Eastern, Northern and Southern States visited this city, nearly all were attracted to his store to buy from his fine stock, or give orders for European books. The literary chit-chat of those men, for I have heard them, reminded me of what can be found in Boswell's "Life of Johnson," where men like the burly, stern moralist Dr. Johnson met the inspired idiot Oliver Goldsmith, Sir Joshua Reynolds, Garrick, and other great men, where their wit and learning kept the table in a roar. Those times are past, but I hope at sometime will be resuscitated. I forget the year when John Pennington removed from Fourth street to Seventh street,

near Walnut street. He was there for several years.
The war broke out in 1861, and as his principal trade
was among Southern men, his business become paralyzed, and his losses great. He felt his loss of the
Southern trade very much; and as New York had
begun about this time to pay special attention to the
importation of books, engravings, and the fine arts, we
lost that part of our business in this city, and it has
been for many years prosecuted with great energy and
tact, and is still pursued with vigor by them. To our
disgrace it must be said, that New York has robbed us
of that fine literary business we had here from 1800 up
to 1860. This city was the great literary emporium
of the United States from 1800 up to 1850. The
finest edition of the Bible — hot-pressed copies —
were issued by the Smalls, and *fac simile* editions of
the English Classics were issued from the press of
Wardle. Nearly all that prestige has gone; spas-
modic attempts appear now and then, it is true, but
the general effect has passed into other hands. John
Pennington died some years ago; his business passed
into the hands of his son, E. Pennington; until physical infirmities caused him to relinquish it into the
hands of his son; but the halo of old John Pennington
has passed away, and his fine old store and name, except to a few, is sunk into oblivion.

PETERSON AND CHILDS.

R. E. Peterson, father-in-law of George W. Childs, commenced the old book business at the northwest corner of Fifth and Arch streets, with Daniels & Smith, about 1848. This partnership did not last very long; Daniels & Smith separated from R. E. Peterson and opened a book store at No. 20 N. Sixth street. This separation, from what cause I know not, produced bad feeling and an intense opposition in the newspapers of the time, especially in the columns of the *Ledger.* By referring to them it will be seen that a fierce opposition was carried on in the press. Mr. Peterson at this time, when opposition ran high, engaged G. W. Childs as a salesman. Mr. Childs at this time was salesman for Mr. Thompson, who kept a bookstore at the northwest corner of Sixth and Arch streets. In a short time the value of the services of Mr. Childs was apparent to Mr. Peterson, and he found he had got a man whose business talents could not be surpassed. He had unbounded energy and a rare discretion.

The old book business cabined and confined this young Hercules, and he desired a larger sphere for his talents, and suggested the publication of books. About this time the intrepid traveler, Dr. Kane, had returned from his Artic voyage—he was the hero of the day.

Mr. Childs saw his golden opportunity, and urged Mr. Peterson to make arrangements with Dr. Kane for the publication of his travels. Mr. Childs, with great energy, entered heart and soul into this great enterprise, and, taking the tide at the flood, pushed it on with a resistless vigor—fanned the flame of excitement from every point that an acute observer only can see—and the result was a marvellous success. The book was illustrated with sketches from Dr. Kane's drawings, by that erratic genius, James Hamilton. Those who are acquainted with art, know well that the genius of James Hamilton, in a collective sense, stands unrivalled as an artist in *chiaroscuro*, and bold effects. The book will always find a place in Arctic discovery, and stands second to none in artistic illustration. I am not sure, but believe that the masterly management of Mr. Childs, in this book caused Mr. Peterson to accept him as his partner.

Many other valuable publications followed this of Dr. Kane.

Judge Bouvier, father-in-law of Mr. Peterson, to whom I have sold many books, was collecting material for his celebrated Law Dictionary, which was published by Childs & Peterson, and took its place at once as a classic law book, and still retains its former position. "American Institutes of Law," by Judge Bouvier, was the second success of author and publishers. R. E.

Peterson made a success of "Familiar Science " by his discreet editorship, and other publications followed in rapid succession.

Among the most noted books in general literature is Allibone's "Dictionary of Authors." I recollect well that a specimen copy was published by the firm and handed around to publishers and booksellers in order to obtain their opinions on it. Mr. Peterson called on me and left one of these copies in order that he should have my opinion. I perused it carefully, and when he again called on me for the copy and my opinion I probably criticised it too plainly. I said then, and repeat it, after thirty years' experience, that it is a book of great value and a monument of industry, but it had then (somewhat remedied since) too much of the mutual admiration society about it, as it gave long critical notices of *living authors* from such sources as *Godey's Magazine, Graham's Magazine,* and others of equal literary value. This opinion did not seem to be appreciated by Mr. Peterson, but I know a great quantity of the matter spoken of did not appear when the book was completed. It was announced to be in one volume, price $5. It was afterwards sold to J. B. Lippincott, and increased to three volumes, royal octavo, and sold at $25. I do not remember whether Childs & Peterson ever completed the one-volume edition or not; but the work stands to-day without

an equal. I know the book is indebted for its existence more to the exertions of Mr. Childs, outside of its
compilation, than to any other man. I believe that
the vast number of books required by Mr. Allibone
to finish the book—that the money required for it—
was furnished by Mr. Childs; and had it not been for
this valuable aid, the world would probably not have
had such a valuable work as it now possesses.

One other work published by this firm I must
mention, as it is the product of a noble woman—the
wife of R. E. Peterson, the daughter of the late Judge
Bouvier, and the mother-in-law of G. W. Childs—
"Familiar Astronomy," 8vo., illustrated.

This firm engaged the learned and able lawyer and
Chief Justice of the Pennsylvania Supreme Court, the
Hon. Judge Sharswood, to edit Blackstone's "Com-
mentaries of the Laws of England." The book to-day
stands as the ablest among our law books. It has
been a source of great profit, both to author and publishers.

I am not sure of the precise time that Mr. Peterson
retired from business, and left it solely in the hands of
Mr. Childs, but it was after Mr. Childs married the
daughter of Mr. Peterson.

The store at Fifth and Arch streets was vacated after
the old book business was closed out, and Mr. Childs
removed to Chestnut street, below Seventh street, east

side, in the second story, and there continued the publications of the old firm.

At this time Mr. Childs published his first almanac [1864], almost similar to the well-known American Almanac published for many years in Boston. This almanac was carefully compiled by Wm. V. McKean, the now accomplished editor of the *Public Ledger*. Mr. Childs showed his usual sagacity in selecting Mr. McKean to superintend his literary bureau, and his good judgment was further confirmed in selecting him as the editor of the *Public Ledger* at the time it was purchased from Mr. Swain by Childs and Drexel. I am not sure how long Mr. Childs carried on his business in Chestnut street; but about 1861, when the war of the Rebellion was opened, he entered into partnership with J. B. Lippincott & Co., the extensive publishers of this city. This partnership did not continue very long, and I presume the cause of it was the purchase of the *Public Ledger* from Mr. Swain by him and Anthony Drexel. The *Public Ledger* was at that time published at the southwest corner of Third and Chestnut streets, and afterwards removed to its present location, southwest corner of Sixth and Chestnut streets. At the time of the purchase of the *Public Ledger* it was issued for *one cent a copy*. The progress of the late war was hastening on, and in its tracks every commodity was raised in price, especially all matters connected with the cotton crop in the South, which was totally cut off from the northern States. Paper of every description was scarce, its rise in price was phenomenal, and as a consequence all newspapers had to increase the price of the daily issue. The *Public Ledger* was raised from *one cent* to its present price, two cents. I will relate an instance of the extraordinary *rise* in the price of old paper. I think it was in 1862 ; I was changing a great part of my old book business into a circulating library, and in order to do this I had a stock of books that must be sold to make room for my library. Old paper was then bringing a high price, *eight cents per pound* with the *covers* on. The book trade was in a state of paralysis, all dull except war articles. I had a very fine collection of old folios and quartos, and many good books, and did not feel like sending them to the paper mill even at that price, *eight cents a pound*. I ordered a furniture car, and in it I sent two tons of books to be sold at auction by Thomas & Son. When I had got the wagon emptied of the books, I went to the office to get an advance of money on them. They very reluctantly said they would like to oblige me, but books were bringing no prices, and they would decline making any advances ; but if so much money would answer (I forget the amount), they would ad-vance it. The sum of money was so small that I

3

ordered the books to be taken away and sent to an old paper store. There I sold them at eight cents per pound, $75 more than Thomas & Son would advance on them. The same kind of books in the same condition to-day, only bring *one-half a cent per pound.*

At the time the *Public Ledger* was bought by Childs and Drexel it was in an effete condition; the late owner had so neglected its interests that it was in a state of coma from paralysis, and it required the energy and push of a Childs to resuscitate it. By the energy and good management of Childs it gradually rose phœnix-like from the ashes of decay, and soon took its position as one of the *first daily family newspapers in the world.* The *Public Ledger* is a family necessity in this city; its high moral tone, its negation of condimented sensationalism, renders it an authority on all the current topics of the day.

W. A. LEARY.

This old bookseller was among the earliest of this century in this city, and is well remembered by the older citizens as being located at Second and New streets. Forty years ago Second street was what Eighth street is now, the chief business street in the city. From South to Poplar street stores of every kind sold their wares—full of energy and life; it was the chief resort for farmers from every part of our suburbs and New Jersey. When the Warnocks *first* commenced an active business in N. Eighth street, about 1848, a new impetus was given to it, and the gradual decay of Second street may be fairly dated from that period.

Mr. Leary was a short, stout man, persevering and industrious in his habits, though by no means an educated man. He dealt in books as a grocer deals in sugar and candles, more by weight than from any intrinsic value; in fact, he did not know anything about the bibliographical qualities of books, he never pretended to know, and for this admission we must accord him due credit.

After he had been fairly successful in selling old books he went into partnership with a Mr. Getz, and begun the publication of books suitable for pedlars—the trade called his books "Leary's Bricks," because they were printed on thick paper and dumpy in appearance. For some years this firm continued selling to pedlars and others, but from some cause it succumbed to a pressure, and the firm went out of existence, leaving no profitable results. Mr. Leary was fortunate in saving some of the wreckage sufficient to live on in a respectable manner. He was a very genial man, and spent the latter years of his life in a very modest manner. He died at a ripe old age a few years ago.

PAINE.

Mr. Paine kept a book store with a book stand on South Second street near Noble street. His stock was not large. He dealt in school books, and sold any old miscellaneous books he could purchase. He was a very kind man, but did not know much about the value of old books.

JOHN CAMPBELL.

He was probably better known among old book buyers than any book-seller of his day. He first commenced a book store at the southeast corner of Sixth and Chestnut streets (State House), about 1849. Previous to this he was a weaver, but always a reader. John was far better educated than any old book-seller of his day. His nature was brusque and fearless, and had the characteristics of his Irish countrymen—acted *first* and thought *afterwards*.

His public life first commenced in England. He was an extreme Chartist and fiery Revolutionist; so active was he among the English Chartists in Manchester, that he was made treasurer of the Chartist Society for all England. Any one by looking over the newspapers of that day will find his name along with Feargus O'Conner, Bronterre O'Brien, and other leaders.

I never heard the precise reason why he suddenly left England for this country: it may have been political. England was in a very feverish state at that time, and many of the Chartists were imprisoned for using seditious language.

When he arrived here he at once pushed with resistless energy into political and religious disputes, and soon became a marked man among the most violent of extremists. Often have I been with him in Societies where extreme views were debated. The slavery question years before the late war was an exciting one, a prolonged and fierce debate was held in the Franklin Hall in South Sixth street near Arch early in the fifties; I took an active interest in it, but John Campbell was the fiery antagonist of the poor African. His views he afterwards elaborated in "*Negromania,*" a violent and one-sided diatribe. The book did not meet with public favor, and was the cause of financial embarrassment. He also published a small book on *Liberty,* the exact title I forget. Its advocacy is strongly in favor of Robespierre and all the French Revolutionists of 1793. His views on religious matters, both written and oral, were very extreme; though brought up a Catholic, he advocated atheism and infidelity in their wildest forms, but after years of more matured experience, he changed his views and died in the faith of the Catholic Church.

His old book business consisted chiefly in law books, and in course of time he acquired a good knowledge of the bibliography of law books. He published a number of new law books, and judging from results, added little either financially or otherwise. Political influence caused him to be removed from Chestnut street, and in connection with Powers he moved to Fifth street above Chestnut street. There he did not continue long, but by political influence he again moved, and was granted the right to locate a book stand in front of the present Custom House, and next to the Western bank. His next move, after a few years—whether from political causes or not—was from there into the basement of what then was the bank of Pennsylvania, and nearly opposite the Custom House. In this basement, about the year 1861, when the late war had fairly commenced, his store became the centre for hot-headed Democrats, who opposed the government in its action in arresting malcontents and opposers of government action. Many arrests were made, and a number of them were imprisoned who became violent in their opposition to the government. Then came the issue of *habeas corpus*. Pamphlets were issued by the dozen in favor of *habeas corpus*. John Campbell's store was the hotbed of this clique of men. Pamphlets were issued from this centre, and it became widely known through the country, and gained the sympathy and encouragement of the Copperheads generally. Campbell had the courage of his opinions, and violently advocated his right and the benefit of his acts. It may be said that this action was in entire harmony with his political career in England. In a short time this *habeas corpus* ceased, and business again ran in the ordinary channels; money became abundant, business became brisk, and the desire for purchasing books increased. Campbell was a pushing man; he soon took the lines of his surroundings, and was one of the heaviest buyers of books at auction. John's burly figure was always expected there, and soon his sonorous voice was heard above all others. If any one chanced to bid against him, woe to the bidder; John would again raise his sonorous voice to a higher pitch, and advance the price in such a vigorous tone that a laugh or a titter would ring through the room. I was once there when a copy—a very fine one—of Dibdin's Bibliomaniac was offered. A fine, scholarly-looking gentleman was there—evidently came to buy this fine copy. He was seated close by John. He had the temerity to bid against him. John turned his lion-like face towards, and scowled at him. John at once bid $5 over the last bid the gentleman made. But he was not to be browbeaten out of his book; another $5 was bid. John bid $5, and it was knocked down to him. I forget the exact price, but it was more than double what it could have been imported from England for. This conduct was his usual one at auction.

It cannot be said that he was, in the fullest sense of the word, a man well posted in book lore, outside of law books. His life was not that of a student, yet possessing a more general knowledge of literature ; but was more of the boisterous politician. His sales of books to his customers were as indiscreet in many cases as the purchase of them at auction. I have seen him, when anxious to make a sale, show his purchase bills to his customer, in order to make the sale.

He removed from the basement of the bank in Chestnut street to Sansom street near Eighth street, where one of his sons still continues the business. Some twenty-five years ago, there was a rage among old book buyers for *Reprints* of old scarce books. John got the fever, and he published some of them ; but ere long the fever died out, and John had many that were left unsold—whether they are all sold now or not I don't know.

There seems to be a time when crotchets appear in almost everything. Crazes or hobbies arise from remote causes. Change in costume is almost universal. South Sea schemes, the rage some years ago for Dutch tulips — all evince some latent instinct in human nature. The book craze for a few years past has been, and still is, fashionable both here and in Europe—the desire for *first editions*. Every cultivated reader knows too well that, in a literary sense, the *first editions* are the most imperfect of any author's work. The reason is plain and obvious: human nature is always imperfect—authors follow the rule, and it is rare when a *second edition* is issued that the imperfections of the author in the *first edition* are not pointed out and altered, and some additions made.

It is to the interest of old booksellers that such senseless crazes exist; but as a true cultivated scholar, his sense of right condemns and censures such useless fancies. It is right that *National Libraries* should collect and store away those precious thoughts, both as to specimens of the immaturity of the author's thoughts and as specimens of workmanship, which varies in every age.

This craze for *first editions* of living authors has arisen since John Campbell died ; had it been in existence during his lifetime, he would have been as deep in it as the most ardent. The craze seems to be passing away for first editions of living authors, at least of mediocre books; but those of men like the divine Shakespeare will ever live and be in demand.

JOHN WOOD.

This old bookseller merits but a short notice. He had his store on South Eighth street, near Jayne street. He had a fair collection of old books for sale, but he knew as much about the character of the books as the books knew about him. He was there for a few years, and succumbed to the pressure of the times. He was an Irishman.

PATRICK LYNCH.

He had a small old book store. He did but little business. He was the agent for the *Boston Pilot*, the chief organ of the Roman Catholics at that time. He was a good fellow, and much respected among his Irish countrymen and others of his faith. Patrick is dead.

HUGH HAMEL.

This old bookseller kept his store on South Tenth street, next to the Mercantile Library. He was there for many years, and had a large and good stock of old books for sale. He had risen from a mere peddler of books, and by dint of perseverance, collected them as a junk dealer collects his rubbish. He was probably the most ignorant of all the old booksellers in this city. At one time he could not write his own name. Whether he acquired this accomplishment afterwards

I know not. He was in appearance a thick-set, low-looking, vulgar Irishman; and it is to be regretted that the latter years of his life were as much devoted to stimulants as to his business. When he died, his business died also.

PETER DOYLE.

He was a man of much culture, with a refined taste; his personal appearance was somewhat peculiar. He was, in physique, rather small; delicate frame, with a large head and a peculiar cast in his eye. His face bore a studious aspect—pale and full of thought. A cast of melancholy, somewhat Hamlet-like, struck you on first impression. He was the most *silent* bookseller I ever met; only his most intimate friends could influence him in any prolonged conversation. He had his books carefully arranged, and when rare or valuable he wrote the most beautiful chirography and suitable descriptions I ever read. He was well posted in general literature, and had a fair knowledge of the bibliographical character of his books. So silent and so very soft in his conversation, that the book had really to sell itself. If you asked for a book and he had it, he would *silently* give it to you and point to the price, which as a rule was higher in price than any other bookseller in the city. No other effort to sell was made. He was always coldly courteous to you, and the reticent gentlemen was always to be seen in him. His window was always filled with choice and rare editions, and often some choice work of art.

The general appearance of his stock of books bore the impress of the connoisseur and refined scholar, and a genuine literary flavor pervaded his whole store. For several years he lived a bachelor's life and kept his store in North Tenth street near the Mercantile Library. It was the resort of the black-letter scholars of his day. I have been informed his name was originally D'Oyley, a French name, and that his family was originally French. This may be so, but it sounds very Irish.

Dr. Evans, dentist, formerly of this city but who for many years has lived in Paris, and became prominently known as dentist to Napoleon the III., and whose conduct and gallantry to the Empress Eugenie when she was fleeing from Paris when the Communists had full sway, and whose life they were seeking like that of her unfortunate predecessor, Queen Antionette, wife of Louis the XVI.—he, Dr. Evans, was by marriage a relative of Peter Doyle, and it is said in the later years of his life that he saw to his comforts. Some few years ago Peter Doyle offered his fine stock of books for sale. Arrangements to this effect were made, and the stock of books were transferred, part in cash and part in notes, to a late bookseller. The notes were partly paid, and Peter Doyle took a part of his stock, a mere remnant, and again opened a store for the sale of old books.

The sale of his fine stock of books was a very unfortunate affair to Peter Doyle, and there can be but little doubt that it hastened the close of his eccentric but high moral life. He was a man easily duped, and many cases are known where designing knaves took advantage of his generosity. One morning he was found dead in his store, unattended and uncared for. Peace to his ashes.

BROWN BROTHERS

Kept for several years an old book store, I think at the northwest corner of Fourth and Arch streets. One of the brothers was employed in the book department of Thomas & Sons, auctioneers, and had the best chances of purchasing old books of any booksellers in the city. This advantage was well used, and enabled the brothers to have a fine collection of books in their store. The brother with Thomas & Sons acquired bad habits—too fond of stimulants—and he died in a few years after the store was opened. The other brother, who was a kind and genial man, after the death of his brother, removed the stock somewhere out in Iowa, and whether he is dead or not I have not heard.

JAMES BARR.

He was a kindly, good man. He kept an old book store with varieties for sale on Market street, near Eleventh street, south side. Here he did a good business; but improvements in building a new store pressed him, and he was compelled to remove. His next store was in Market street, near Tenth street, and 'here sold old books and new ones. He was a sincere Methodist, and sold Methodist books, and also stationery. The latter years of his life were very chequered ones, and he died poor, but highly respected.

JOSEPH SABIN.

When I first knew Joseph Sabin it was in 1848; he was then a salesman for Appleton & Co., in their store on Chesnut street below Seventh street, south side. The *first* book imported from England was through him. The Appletons, about 1850, removed their stock to New York, and I suppose Sabin went with them. How long he continued with them I know not; he was for several years in New York, and about 1860, or previous to that year, he came to my store, then 218 S. Eighth street, and, in his usual saturnine manner, asked me if I thought another old book store in this city would succeed. I said that depended on so many conditions that I could not answer that question. . He then said he had a store in New York city, and purposed to move the stock here. He did so, and opened a store in what was called then Hart's building, in Sixth street above Chestnut street. I went to see his stock of old books, but they were not remarkable either in quantity or in quality.

He entered into his new store with vigor and energy, and soon became the chief buyer at Thomas and Son's auction store. For a few years he and John Campbell were the principal buyers, and few buyers could purchase books except Sabin and Campbell. Jennings the auctioneer seemed to favor them when opportunity offered. The consequence was that as credit was freely given, Sabin soon had a fine stock of books, the finest in the city at that time. Sabin was the connoisseur among old book buyers, and a fine business was the result. Had his rectitude been equal to his ability, none could have surpassed him in his business. One fine morning his store was closed and his whereabouts was not known. Jennings, of Thomas & Son's, who had credited him with several thousand dollars, was soon on the alert, and found all the books had been shipped to New York. He at once went there, replevined them, and had them sent to their auction store and sold on their account. This ended Sabin's career in this city. He remained in

New York, commenced the auction business, and
failed in that. His next move was, he bought an old
book store out in Nassau street, and for many years
did well. He was the chief authority among old
buyers, and well he deserved the opinion of all in that
line. His business was so large that he could not fail
to have made a fortune even with the commonest
prudence. He became *the* authority on all important
book sales. He sold the celebrated library of W. E.
Burton and other well-known libraries. In fact, if
an important sale of books in New York took place,
Sabin was the man that was engaged to compile the
catalogue and manage the sale. He was thoroughly
competent to do this, and the amount of money he
made in ten years must have been sufficient to keep
his family in fair condition, but alas! it did not.
Where it went none knows.

Some years ago he commenced to collect matter
for an American Bibliography. Rich's "*American
Bibliography,*" and Stevens' "*Nuggets,*" are excellent
books, indispensable for the American student; but
like all other books of this class, very deficient. This
idea of Sabin's is a good one. He started his "*American Bibliography*" and published it in volumes. It is
not yet finished. He obtained subscriptions for it
and got many. Trubner of London had a lawsuit
with him about this book. He seemed to have the

faculty of creating wrangles with every one he had
business with, and I presume this was the cause of him
losing the vast amount of money he had made in his
legitimate business.

His Dictionary of America is valuable in collecting
from all sources whatever that has appeared published
on America; but the useless remarks, unscholarly
criticism, and a malevolent and saturnine spirit per-
meate the whole of the volumes, destroy the valuable
portion, and produce a certain nausea among those
that are likely to use it. If Sabin had taken for his
models such men as Brunet or Lowndes, his book
would have been admired by bibliographers rather
than censured.

The issue of this book caused several lawsuits.
Trubner and Quaritch of London were involved, and
large sums of money were lost in the contest. Failure
after failure were the consequences of his conduct, and
it is to be regretted that some of his sons, who aro
now selling books in London, have suffered from such
erratic management.

Joseph Sabin was an Englishman, and from his
youth brought up as a bookseller. I have stated that
when a young man he was a salesman in this city for
the Appletons. He had rare business tact, a love for
old books, more in a mercantile sense than for possessing any general knowledge of their contents. He was

4

not a cultured man, and therefore not a reading man. He could not shine in literary conversation, but you would admire him for his vast fund of *catalogue knowledge*, a skeletonized idea of what books contained.

SCANLAN.

He was a clear-headed and conscientious man, an Irishman by birth, and had a fair knowledge of English literature. He was an earnest man, with very strong Roman Catholic views on religion. Though seemingly tolerant to others who differed with him, yet below the surface you could see mirrored the Catholic of the middle ages. He had a select stock of good books chiefly reflecting the opinions of the Roman church. He had a specialty in Spanish books, and his store on Fifth street below Chestnut was well known to the book hunter. He retired from business and died a few years ago.

MOSES POLOCK.

He was brought up in the business of book-selling in the now extinct firm of McCarthy & Davis, at their store in Market street near Fourth street, north side. McCarthy retired from the firm some years before Davis brothers died, whom I knew well as fine specimens of business men of former years. This firm published many fine books, British Drama, Shake-speare, and many law books. Their chief business was wholesale, and was successful in making money. Moses Polock became their chief business man, and when the Davis's died, he was made their executor, a great compliment for a young man not more than 30 years of age. He was instructed to close the business, and I recollect well that the stock of books, which were very large, were sold at auction by Thomas & Sons, when they occupied the *now rear* end of Wana-maker's store, southeast corner of Sixth and Market streets. The stock was very large, but it was all sold except what Moses Polock bought in, and with this stock of books he commenced the old book business in Commerce street below Fifth street (second story), where he still can be found. His store is well filled with many rare books, which he has unpreten-tiously and quietly added the last forty years. Some years ago he published Brockden Brown's works in seven volumes, the *first American novelist;* but I am inclined to think as a business speculation it was a failure. The library of Professor Reed, who was lost in the steamer Arctic over thirty years ago, he bought of the family, and in it were many fine books. The Roxborough Club books, a rare collection of early English reprints, were in this library. I presume Moses Polock was and is in a fair comfortable condi-

tion, because he made little exertion as a business
man to sell his books, and because his prices are and
were always fanciful. At any time after 10 o'clock
in the morning you can ascend to his store; there you
will find him bachelor-like all alone in his glory,.
breathing the atmosphere of his old books. He will
meet you in the most genial manner, and will talk to
you about his gems in ˙the most intelligent spirit.
There is but one exception I know of to this. He
once sold for $16 "The Laws of New York,"
printed by W. Bradford, a good price at that time;
but the same copy was sold in the Brindley's Collection of Americana at auction for $1600. The men-
tion of this fact operates· on Polock's mind as if he
had taken bitter gall for his breakfast. He has a rare
early knowledge of men in the book business for the
last forty years; but being a very reticent and diffi-
dent man, I am afraid those of the city will lose a
charming lot of history about book-sellers, publishers
and books. He is still in his old place, ever ready to
do business with you, but is seldom visited except
some old book-worm wants some very scarce book or
pamphlet.

JOHN HUNT.

Some twenty-five years ago, this brusque Englishman kept a book stand at the southeast corner of

Sixth and Arch streets, and was very energetic and pushing in business. He also peddled books through the country in a wagon. He seemed to do a thriving business for several years; but all is not gold that glitters. His stock was seized and sold for the benefit of his creditors. He still lives in Camden, N. J.

JARRETT.

This energetic Englishman had a book stand at the northeast corner of Sixth and Market streets for a few years. His stock of books were few in number, and many of them were sold on commission. He did not keep the store very long, but afterwards went to the present Leary's book store in Ninth street near Market street; and there for several years he could be found at the outside stand selling books. In appearance he was of small stature, nervous in his actions, but accommodating in his manners. He was a man of more than average intellect, always fond of books, and his long experience in selling them gave him a large amount of book knowledge which was always presented free gratis to every book buyer. He died a few years ago.

EMANUEL PRICE (PETER PEPPERCORN).

To omit to portray this singular character among the galaxy of old-book sellers, would be as absurd as

acting the play of Hamlet without the personnel of
Hamlet.   It is over forty years ago when I first knew
him ; he was then porter in a wholesale drug store on
Market street above Sixth street, north side.   He then
had just arrived from England, and he has told me
since that when he came here he had a very limited
education—he could read, but not write.   He saw the
importance and value of writing, even in his humble
position of porter, and he resolved to learn· to write ;
and the use of his caustic pen is well known in our
newspaper literature.   During the late civil war his
doggerel rhymes were well known for their bitterness
and causticity.   He wrote a parody on Sheridan's ride
which he acknowledged literally killed him.   He was
a modern Hudibras, and cut and slashed everything
and every one that he deemed worthy of notice.   His
various lucubrations have been collected and printed
and published in one volume by Rees, Welsh & Co.,
the law booksellers on South Ninth street, above
Chestnut street.   The chief value of the book consists
in its being a sardonic satire of the times.   Wit and
humor flashes out of it here and there, that some future local historian may quote a century hence.

I do not remember the year, nor the store where he
first began selling books, but it may be not less than
fifteen years ago.   Then he was with Rees Welsh &
Co., who at that time sold miscellaneous and law

books. This firm soon found that he was to them a
very valuable man, and he was given the chief position in the store. He was their chief buyer for many
years, and discharged his duties well and faithfully.
He soon acquired by experience and his quickness of
intellect a rare knowledge of books, second to none in
any book store in this city. I do not know of one
old-book seller in this city that is his equal in the
general knowledge of books. He possesses a varied
fitness for such a position; he is pleasant in his address; sometimes too querulous in his conversation,
but always very entertaining when talking about
books.

When I first knew him his penchant was botany.
In his spare hours from his work he would go into the
fields, then in the suburbs of the city, away down into
the Neck, as it is called; there he would feast on the
various plants, and collect them for his herbarium.
Few men know the botany of this city equal to Price,
but his botanical peregrinations, especially on a Sun-
day, would carry him into New Jersey and for many
miles around the environs of this city. The local botanical literature of this city is at his finger ends, far
surpassing any one I know.

While pursuing botany with such ardor—nay, pas-
sion—he was struck with the varieties of the insect
world; he saw that nature in her productions was as

manifold in her varieties and as munificent in her grandeurs here, as she is with the flowers in nature's garden and in her ever-varied products in the field. He studied insect life, and is quite an adept in this special branch of study.

I have only given a cursory notice of the abilities of this self-educated man, but sufficient, I trust, to show that any man pursuing the self-denial and possessing the *will* to do, as he has shown in his life-work, can be a more useful man than men generally are. I regret to say that he is very poor and in indigent circumstances, arising from peculiar idiosyncrasies that have made his usefulness almost nil. Good chances he has had to be in his old age very comfortable, but his peculiar passions—impractical in business—have made his services not desirable. He is still about the city, picking up old books and selling them where he can. He preserves still a certain degree of independence and self-respect which are more characteristic of the Englishman than any other nationality.

REES WELSH & CO.

This firm first commenced the old-book business in Walnut street below Fifth street, and there dealt chiefly in old law books. In a short time they added miscellaneous books, and both being young men, they were energetic in their actions. They did not stay

long on Walnut street, but removed to South Ninth
street, above Chestnut street, into the store now
occupied as an old book store by McKay. Price
was engaged by them as their chief buyer, and was
with them for several years, and they did an active
business. In the course of events the partnership was
dissolved. Rees Welsh moved his stock where he
now is, a few doors above the old store. He sold off
his miscellaneous books, and devoted himself to the sale
of old law books, and is also the publisher of many
law books. He is still in the same store, and carries
on the selling of old law books and law book publisher.

H. McKEAN.

This old book-seller, who had a book stand against
the burial ground was in Fifth street, near Spruce;
and also a book store at the northwest corner of Fifth
and Adelphi streets—added but little to the credit of
the profession of old booksellers. He was literally of
the character of an old junk dealer; and as a man his
conduct was anything but exemplary—nay, censurable
in every sense. I regret to write thus, but truth is
the best, after all cavil may say. He was an Irishman
by birth, but is now dead.

W. S. RENTUOL.

An odd-looking character, a Scotchman by birth,

and a good type of the old curiosity monger. He is lean and lanky in personal appearance, and always very frowsy-looking about the head. He has a fine collection of old Presbyterian books, and is located in the second story on Sixth street above Market. I understand he came here from Pittsburgh. He has been in this city selling old Presbyterian books for over thirty years, but is known only by that class of book-buyers. He is of the old blue-stocking type, which is now becoming rare. I presume that from his long experience he knows every book of note in the literature he sells, from John Knox to the Old Covenanters of to-day. He is known to few collectors of books, as he deals only in those mentioned.

BARDSLEY.

This old bookseller died a few years ago. He kept a book stand at the southeast corner of Sixth and Minor streets. His stock was not large, but he kept a fair class of books. He was kind and genial in his manners. He did not boast of having any special knowledge of books; he was a mere vendor. A few years ago he sold out his books and accepted the position of selling outside, at the stand of Leary's book store. He was a man well respected. While engaged at the book stand he suddenly died. He was an Englishman by birth.

W. A. LEARY, JR.

He was the son of W. A. Leary, whom I have de-scribed. He went to the war. When it was over, he started in the old book business. First he peddled books in a basket; then he afterwards had a very small book stand on Water street, on the wharf, I think, near Walnut street. He was full of energy and pluck. He persevered, and in a short time rented the store on the southeast corner of Fifth and Walnut streets. His business increased, and he soon became an active old bookseller. He was a mere vender of books; he neither knew their contents nor cared to know. He did not profess to be even a catalogue old bookseller, but bought cheap and sold at a good profit. He succeeded in a few years to amass a large collection of old books; but success with him, like with many others, destroyed those business habits necessary to continued success, and stimulants ended his career. He died several years ago. The business was sold out for $5,000, and C. Mann and E. Stuart were the purchasers. W. A. Leary, Jr., was a man of middle stature, nothing prepossessing in his appearance, gruff and blunt in his address. His education was not above the ordinary standard; he was a common man, but his tact and energy were above the average.

CRAWFORD.

In the basement of Edwards' building, in Walnut street below Sixth street, this old bookseller commenced business with a small stock. By economy and perseverance he soon acquired a good stock of books, and in a few years relinquished the old book trade and commenced buying old stereotype plates, and jobbed in that business. He has for a few years past occupied a store in Ninth Street, near Arch Street, and still continues jobbing in new books.

JORDAN BROTHERS.

These two young men commenced to sell old books some twelve years ago in South Seventh street, near Sansom street, on the west side. The store was a small one, and their stock was small. In a few years, by their energy, perseverance and economy, they found more room was required. The respected John Pennington's store became vacated—which is nearly opposite their first store—and they removed into it, giving them ample room for more books. I presume they removed, after being there a short time, on account of dullness in business; at any rate their trade fell off, and they rented a store in Market street, above Seventh street, and there got fairly into busi· ness again. The property was sold, and bought by the present Penn Township Bank, and they were noti-

fied to leave. They then removed to South Ninth
street, above Market street, and in· a short time removed again to their present location, South Ninth
street, above Race, east side. They have a fair stock
of old books, and are always on the alert at auction
sales and other places where books are for sale. They
are both young men, and like young men in general,
their enthusiasm and pluck often are in excess of prudence and knowledge. They are not in mental culture above the average of men, nor are they book
lore men in any sense of the word, yet they are am-
bitious, and strive hard to become well posted up in
book lore. They probably are among the best catalogued book sellers in the city, and so far merit encouragement. Time will do more for them in smooth-
ing down their unevenness and youthful extravagances
in their habits and methods, than any other process
could accomplish. I would encourage them onwards
—they are on the right track—but in order to be
more efficient, read the best authors; there is no royal
road to knowledge; consult Lowndes and Brunet for
a better acquaintance with the history of books.

THOMAS.

This old book-seller has been in his present location,
Ninth street above Race street, for over ten years.
He began the old book business in a very humble

way, but by dint of perseverance and having a better
knowledge of books by reason of his superior mental
culture, has surpassed both in numbers and quality
most of his rivals. I am not personally acquainted
with him, but I learn from others who are that he is
from New Jersey, and having a literary taste, he came
here and very naturally mixed himself among books
and booksellers. I am told he occasionally writes
for the magazines and other papers, and possesses a
good general knowledge of literature. He had a
coterie of literary men meeting at his store, and there
reading essays and debating on literary subjects.
This method of becoming a general adept on belles-
lettres is highly commendable, and ought to be more
generally adopted. It is to be much regretted that
this manner of conducting business is not more generally adopted by our old book-sellers; it is a method
that raises and elevates the character of the old-book
trade. I do not know of a single old-book seller in
this city who has shown the capacity and desire that
this Thomas has so far shown. I do not know of one
of them who has the ability of rendering to their profession a modicum of literary work, but are mere
venders of books. Thomas, I am informed, has not
only a fine collection of old books, but he has specu-
lated in mining, and I hope has made more money in
it than in selling old books. It is a rare thing that any

old-book seller can do more than make a comfortable
living—I mean who has *exclusively* devoted himself
to selling *old books*. There are some who started as
old-book sellers, and who are mere venders of books,
like the grocer sells a pound of candles; but when
money is made by them, it is only as *book jobbers* or
publishers. In a mere utilitarian sense it is right,
but an old-book seller who loves his books and their
authors, and who can'descant on their lives and re-
hearse the subject matter of their books, and who can
render his literary society enjoyable by talking about
Shakspeare or Boswell's Life of Johnson and the
"musical glasses" this is the true man to his profession, and one who enlists my sympathies and gains
my admiration.

HENRY HOLLOWAY.

I find that this person suggests to me, that when I
said "Thomas is the *only* old bookseller I know who
had any literary capacity," I made an error—this
man Holloway must be included. He commenced
the old-book business some twenty years ago in S.
Tenth street near Market street, east side. He was
previous to this a teacher, and begun chiefly in school
books, and afterwards added general literature. For
some years he was very successful; his stock so increased that he rented the next store, and had both of

them well filled with books. He is a man of general culture, and has translated books from the German. In physique he is weak and puny; he has been suffering for over twenty years from a spinal complaint, but he still lives and sells old books; he is kind and genial in his manners, and a very interesting conversationalist. I have sold him many books in the course of twenty years, and always found him pleasant. After he had taken the additional store in Tenth street, he flourished for some time; but some ill luck or misfortune overtook him, and he had to remove to S. Ninth street, near Cherry street. There he opened with a poor stock of books; he lingered there for a short time, and then he removed to Eighth and Wood streets, with very few books, and opened a newspaper stand, where he remained a few years doling out a mere existence. About a year ago he removed to S. Tenth street, above Walnut, and there he has a few books, and I hope is improving his financial condition. Old age is creeping on him, and with it poor health: it is not to be wondered at that he should be somewhat eccentric in his habits.

LEARY & CO. (E. S. STUART & Co.).

The present proprietors of this store bought it from the widow of W. A. Leary, jr., when it was at the southwest corner of Fifth and Walnut streets. E. S.

Stuart was in the employ of Leary, jr., from a boy, and was apt, industrious and intelligent. He was the chief person on whom Leary, jr., depended, and mainly attended to the business during the latter years of Leary's life, which were chiefly spent outside of his store. His conduct was noticed, and gained the admiration of his customers, chief among whom was Charles Mann. He admired Stuart for his personal attention to business and the kindness and urbanity he displayed.

At the death of Leary, jr., the business was for sale. Stuart not having the money to buy, it was arranged that C. Mann and Stuart should buy it, and a co-partnership was formed under the name of Leary & Co. The business is continued by the above firm with energy and good management. Stuart infused new energy into the business, and with its former impetus it soon outgrew the dimensions of the store. More room was required, and Mann bought the present property, No. 9 South Ninth street.

Under the good and spirited management of Stuart the business progressed very rapidly, so that now it has one of the largest stocks of old and new books in the country. Large additions to the store have been made, and still the cry is "more room."

The business is now somewhat diverted from the original business carried on by Leary, jr. Then it

5

was purely old books, now it is old and new books, and new book jobbing forms a large portion of the business. Old and new school books are a specialty. A business of the kind carried on by such a store embraces the purchase of all kinds of books, and it is somewhat singular that the large number of books purchased, many of them good ones—that out of this large business, the only specialty or chief one is the lowest type in the old book business. Old booksellers everywhere consider old school books as trash, and place them away in some remote corner of the store. I am aware that the plea is, there is money in them; I am also aware that this firm has made some money out of them; hence it is continued. But does not this show that the prevailing active spirit of this firm is not influenced by such high types as James Lackington, Henry Bohn or a Quaritch, or the first-class old booksellers in Europe and in this country? All persons who know this well-known store know that it contains many first-class books; and why the lowest class should be their specialty can only be accounted for on the plea of making money. Primarily speaking, money is the chief factor, the great lever in business; but there were old booksellers, and there are still a few left, who look on money produced as secondary as a means to a brighter and nobler end. That end is the intrinsic love of the subject-matter of the books—the large amount of knowledge derived from the reading of them—the association and communion with the great minds of the past and the present—all of which tend to elevate the mind, the development of a higher moral tone, and the pleasures of intellectual growth. I know of old booksellers who have on their shelves the finest and *recherche editions* of the best authors. I have been in their stores when some of those fine books have been sold, and when the buyer had gone the expression was made, "I am sorry I have sold that book—such a fine edition of so great a writer." Such men are rare, I know, and show that the money value of the book was merely secondary. This trend of thought leads to the conclusion that the able executive ability which controls it, is more *objective* in its views than *subjective* in its aspirations. This firm has the largest collection of old books for sale in this city, and I hope no other outside influences will ever deprive it of its enviable position. Local pride is a great virtue, and narrow must be the aspirations of any one who does not feel a proper pride in such local institutions. These efforts reflect honor and dignity on their owners.

HOLLOWAY.

I know but little of this old bookseller, except that he is a brother to Henry Holloway, whom I have noticed.　He has a book stand and basement in Third street, near Walnut, and has been there for several years, and has a stock of old books and magazines jumbled up in a very chaotic mass.

JOHN KING.

He is in a small store in South Tenth street, above Walnut, and has a small and miscellaneous lot of books.

WALTER B. SAUNDERS

Was until recently on South Tenth street, above Chestnut, east side; he had the *two stores* made into *one*.

In *quality* he had the finest and most valuable stock of old books in this city, though not in quantity.　His books were chiefly medical and scientific. The finest and most costly editions could be seen in his windows—folios on natural history and other scientific works, fine English and foreign editions, illustrated most sumptuously.

Saunders is one of the most courtly and polished of all our old booksellers.　He is well educated, and knows the character of the books he has for sale.

A few months ago he removed his fine stock of books into a large store in Walnut street, above Ninth street, and I learn he is selling off his fine books and has commenced the publication of medical books. For this I am sorry, and I fear it shows that the patronage of our book buyers has not been liberal enough to induce him to continue to have for sale such a fine class of books.

SCHAFFER & KORADIE

Are German booksellers at Fourth and Wood streets. They had some time ago a large collection of old German books for sale, and imported books to order.

It is a most singular fact that in this city, with a German population of over 300,000, they sustain only *one* that deals in old books, and this on a small scale. This fact reflects on the generally well educated German but little credit. Why this should be so I do not know. I have asked well educated Germans about this deplorable fact, but no good solution can be given. Some say that the educated German cannot be found here, or at least but few of them, their chief object in life is work, smoke and drink lager beer, and only read their newspapers. I am sorry to say that there is a great deal of truth in this partial explanation. Let us hope this state of things will be changed.

C. J. PRICE.

This bookseller has had a varied career, both in old and new books. When I first knew him, some thirty years ago, he had a book store on Sixth street, above Chestnut street, east side, in what was then called Hart's building: it was owned by Abraham Hart. I have understood that Mr. McElroy, the publisher of the City Directory at that time, furnished the money. Price had a fine class of art books, and devoted himself to that class of literature. I recollect that he was the agent in this country for the "Royal Gallery," a fine royal folio, filled with the finest engravings of copies from Turner, Stanfield, and other first-class living artists of England. This book had deservedly a large sale—books of this character he imported, and had a valuable stock. Business embarrassments caused the stock to be sold at Thomas & Sons' auction store. After this I think he went as salesman to Appleton's book store in New York. He did not stay in New York very long, but opened a book store in Sansom street, near Eighth street, and I think Willis P. Hazard was in partnership with him. This business was closed for what reason I know not; he then went as salesman to Porter & Coates' book store; there he remained for several years. He left Porter & Coates and opened a room in the building where he now is, as agent for the purchase of foreign books; he has a large knowledge of fine English books.

DAVID McKAY.

This young man, whom I am not personally acquainted with, I have learned is a Scotchman, and
was a salesman in Lippincott's book store. He started
the old and new book business a few years ago, and
seems full of energy. His stock of new and old books
is large and of good quality. His experience in old
books is necessarily limited, and as several of our old
booksellers have become venders and jobbers of new
books, it can scarcely be expected that this young
man, who is a large jobber of new books, can be of
much authority among bibliomaniacs. He also pub-
lishes a few books, and judging from their character,
no great fortune can be expected from their sales.
His store is on Ninth street above Chestnut street,
rear of the Girard House.

W. H. BROTHERHEAD.

His place of business is at 288 Girard avenue. He
has been selling old books for a year, and seems as if
success was with him. He has a full stock, and I
trust all will be successful. He is one of my sons,
and I trust and believe that the old book business will
prosper.

MEN AND BOOKS.

KNOWLEDGE of books is the great distinctive quality between man and the brute. Here the line of demarcation can be plainly drawn, and the value of knowledge clearly seen. Books are the greatest factors in modern civilization; they are the vehicles whereby man communicates with man, and are the creators and generators of all that is noble and valuable. To the religious and devout thinker they are a solace and a pleasure; to the novelist who aspires to generalize human actions and movements they are indispensable; to the deep, profound metaphysician they are wells of truth inexhaustible—and probed by men like Kant, Herbert Spencer and John Stuart Mill, hidden truths still are there to be more fully explored; to the historical scholar they present new unexplored mines of wealth, that have been buried in the ruins of Nineveh and Babylon—such as are exhibited in the British Museum, in the Elgin Marbles, and in the books of Layard and others. That glorious and magnificent book of Lord Kingsbury on the Mexican Antiquities, grand as it is, has

only touched the surface; when the hieroglyphical
language of the ancient Aztecs, which abound in the
architectural remains of these countries, finds a Cham-
pollion to fully translate this language as he translated
the Egyptian, then one of the darkest and most remote
of nations will be disclosed to view. History is even
unfolding itself in the confirmation of biblical truths
by a Smyth or a Tischendorf; the ruins of Rome and
Pompeii of late years have gratified the historical student through the medium of books, and enhanced the
value of knowledge to mankind. The glorious crea-
tions of Shakspeare and the whole of the Elizabethan
age of literary giants would have been but little known
except through the medium of books. No pen can
adequately describe the pleasures they have given and
are giving to countless millions. The scientific man
is indebted more to the literature of books than to
personal observation; few can delve into the bowels
of the earth and luxuriate amongst its strata, and pile
up fossils of every description, and bring forth the results in their sanctums—like a Lyell, a Darwin, a
Huxley, or a Tyndale. The many who are called
scientific thinkers—and able ones, too—derive their
knowledge more from books than actual observation.
The litterateur and the journalist, to whom we owe so
much of our pleasure in every-day life, feed exclusively on the literary pabulum in books.

The novel writers, with few exceptions, are only the reflex of our common life.   Scott, Bulwer, Dickens, George Eliot and Thackeray have more than given us a reflex of common life; they have presented to us life-like characters of the past and present that will never perish.   George Eliot has done more than that; she has penetrated the depths of human reason, and has given us such a masterly analysis of human passions that they are Shakespearian in their breadth and depth.   All these writers have produced books that are so subjective in their character that all thinkers are delighted with them.

Books to the politician and statesman are their daily food for thought and reflection; paste and scissors are essential, and scraps of thought are picked up everywhere and rendered subservient to their ends.

The preacher, no matter to what church he belongs, whether he is a St. Augustine, a Chillingworth, or a Clarke, is a great thinker and creator of religious thought.   Without the products of such minds, that are to be found only in books, what would the modern divine do?   A few men like Spurgeon and Beecher who create thought would live—but the majority of our divines would lapse into nothingness. The ideas of these men are principally derived from greater minds, and the products of such minds can only be found in books.   Books to such minds are what tools are to carpenters—indispensable.

PRICES AND EDITONS OF BOOKS.

IN connection with my reminiscences, I deem it will be of some value to present and future old book buyers to place on record the prices books brought years ago from my own sales and those sold at auction. In one of my importations of English old books, I had the two volumes of Josslyn's voyages made in 1633–4. They are small 12mo. volumes, and when I sold them for $2.50 each, I thought I had obtained a good price: now these volumes would bring $50.

Jefferson, when U. S. Minister to France, *first* published his "Notes on Virginia," 1782: he presented nearly all of his copies to friends and literary men whom he knew. On the fly-leaf, next to the title page, he accompanied the book with a few autographic lines suitable to the person to whom he gave the copy. Thus the *first edition* is very rare, and is enhanced in value by his autographic remarks. I bought a copy and sold it to a collector in this city for $5.50. I thought it then a large price, but now it would probably bring $50.

Forty years ago, Franklin's *imprints* were much more plentiful than now, and I have sold many of them at $1.00 each. Once I had a very fine copy of Logan's translation of "Cato Major," printed by Franklin, and sold it for $2.50—a fancy price I considered it then, but it has since brought $50.

When I sold autographs, in one of my visits to Richmond, Virginia, I bought of a lady one of the finest autograph letters of Washington I ever saw, and I have seen many and sold many; it was a love letter in four pages quarto, with his name in full in *three* different parts of the letter. He wrote this letter to Bessie Fairfax, who was the go-between for him and Mrs. Custis. When Washington was surveying in different parts of the State of Virginia, he took this method of cementing his affections, and thus securing Mrs. Custis for his wife. I offered this letter for sale, but the autograph mania had then cooled—none here would pay $100 for it. I then offered it at auction; it was well advertised; the most loving parts of the letter were freely printed in the *New York Herald;* the price was limited to $100; no better price could be obtained than $35; it was withdrawn. In 1878 I was compelled by sickness to travel in England; I took the letter with me, knowing well I could sell it there. I went to see my friend Wm. Naylor, a gentleman of means, now dead, and who dealt in autographs for pastime. I showed him the letter; he was in ecstacies with it, and asked the price; I said £20; he said, "Leave it with me, I can sell it;" I did so; in a few days he wrote me and paid me the money. The fluctuation in the price of books is as various as in the sale of autographs. In the sale of gentle John Allan, of New York, who was a good customer of mine, a letter of Washington's was sold; the competition was intense, and it sold for $3,000. It was afterwards proven that Mr. Allan had bought this of a man who had stolen it from the city archives of New York. The city claimed it; a law-suit was the re-sult, and the claimant, the city of New York, recovered it.

I bought from the heirs of Charles Thomson, Secretary for the First Congress of the United States, a unique copy of the Constitutions of the thirteen Colonies—then States—and printed by order of Congress. This copy had an extra Constitution, I think, of Maine. The book in any condition is rare; it was bound in boards. This copy was the one used by Charles Thomson, and on the side was written in large text *Charles Thomson.* There being no doubt of its authenticity, I sent it to Mr. Spofford, Librarian of the National Library, in Washington. I thought this historical relic would be highly prized, and should have been placed among Revolutionary books. A full description was given, and Mr. Spofford replied and stated that as he was not authorized to pay such a price—$50—it had to go before the Library Committee. It was there for some weeks, and the answer returned was that $15 was offered! This copy was returned, and was afterwards sold to James Lenox, and it can be seen in his valuable library in New York. This book should have been in the National Library, and would be there had it not been left to the decision of politicians.

In 1857 the Rev. Dr. Boardman, of this city, engaged me to collect for James Lenox, of New York, all the *different American editions* of the Bible, both Catholic and Protestant. Special instructions were given to buy the Bible authorized by Congress, and printed by Aitkin in 1782. This Bible is a small 12mo. It is bound in sheep, and sometimes in two volumes, but oftener in one. I advertised in the newspapers for it. After a few days several imperfect copies were brought, which I did not buy; but a very fine copy was offered, and I paid for it $25—this was the price I offered to pay in my advertisements. I collected for James Lenox a large number of Bibles, and I presume the fine collection which is now in the Lenox Library in New York were bought by me for him. It is not out of place here to state that though the Aitkin's Bible bears the date 1782—the

earliest American imprint of the Bible—it is stated
by Lowndes, the eminent English bibliographer, that
the Bible bearing the London imprint 1752, was
printed in Boston for Mark Baskett.

In these recollections and experiences of mine, I desire to place on a more permanent record the results of
some of the sales of many of our best libraries of eminent collectors, which were realized at auction sales.

The first is the fine library of E. B. Corwin, that
was sold in November, 1856. The old bookseller
and collector will find very valuable data that will be
of invaluable use in researches for rare books and
their value. In this and other sales which I shall in-
clude, it will be seen that *prices* fluctuate but little,
and the general tendency is upward.

The old bookseller and collector will here find sufficient evidence to lay the flattering unction to his
soul that if this hobby or true literary taste of his is
a costly affair, he can, with a fair knowledge of
literature and using good discretion, spend his thousands of dollars in such a way that the capital sum of
money he has spent is in many cases realizing a good
interest. In a mere money point of view—and that
is ignoble—his investments will average a larger interest than is generally acquired in mercantile pursuits. This opinion is not intended to vitiate or in
any way to decry other pursuits in the various activ-

ities of life, but to show the few who are sufficiently cultured in general literature that the spare time they have from their general business is a credit to them. They elevate the literary taste of the nation, raise its standard to the world, and show to the nations that though we are creating a new world of industries out of a howling wilderness, yet our inherited tastes incline us and show that the subjective part of our nature crops out and illustrates the fact that Americans by their fine libraries are deserving, at least in England, of it being said that they are the choicest of buyers of books, and by their purchases have materially raised the prices in English markets. But how much more consoling it is to the cultured American book buyer, when he compares his purchases of books, the money he has spent on them, with the money spent by the roue, the club man, the sensualist, the gambler or the sportsman?

The *mere* pleasure of *collecting* books is an ecstatic one, even if the contents are not read; how much more creditable it is to say that John Smith has a fine library—it carries with it a thousand pleasant associations — and then compare him with John Jones, who is a dude in dress, a great club man, boasts of how many bottles of champagne he drank last night, of the young girls he has ruined; see him parading Chestnut Street in the latest style of dress, a

cane in his hand, casting his leering wicked eyes on
the ladies that are promenading. Follow him through
a few years you will find a physical wreck, filled with
disease of almost every kind, rheumatism, gout, Bright's
disease and others of a more poisonous nature, and at
last he prematurely dies, leaving a wretched record of
a life thrown away. The book collector when he
dies leaves the results in his fine library, which if it
does not realize at sale the amount of its original cost
it leaves money for use to his family, whose surroundings are a blessing and a credit to all.

The first sale of memorable books I shall print is
that of E. B. Corwin's, of New York.

SALE OF THE LATE E. B. CORWIN'S LIBRARY.

(*From the Publisher's Circular.*)

This very fine and choice collection was sold by
Messrs. Bangs, Brother & Co., during the middle of
November, 1856. The prices obtained have been quite
large, and the bidding for rare books very spirited.
Among others which we have marked are "The
Boston Chronicle" for 1768, *with many supplements
and extraordinary papers*, 4to., $7 — rather cheap;
"Monster of Monsters, by Th. Thumb, Esq.," Bost.
1754, a rare tract, $5 ; some New York City Direc-
tories from 1800, $2 each ; a Philadelphia Directory,
1785, $3.50; (I have sold this 1785 Directory for
$12;) "R. L., a Letter of Advice to a Young Gen-

6

tleman leaving the University," New York, 1696, $12.50; the "Timepiece and Literary Companion," edited by Philip Freneau, from No. 1, March 13, 1797, to No. 79, September 11, $7.50; "Virginia Gazette, *with the freshest advices*," $16; "Bibliography, a Poem, in six Books," 8vo., Lond. 1812, very rare, only fifty copies having been printed, $2.50, less than had been expected; a copy of the "Bibliotheca Americana," Lond. 1789, a very scarce book, attributed to various authors, $10.25; "Bibliothecæ Americanæ Primordia; an Attempt towards laying the Foundation of an American Library, in several Books, Papers and Writings, presented to the Society for the Propagation of the Gospel," by White Kennet, 4to, London, 1713, highly thought of by collectors, brought only $16; a large paper copy, uncut, of Dibdin's "Bibliomania," of which only fifty-five copies were printed, $17; a number of Dibdin's boooks were sold for rather moderate prices; Ludewig's "Literature of American Local History; a Bibliographical History," N. Y., 1846, $6; a large paper copy, uncut, of the "Bibliotheca Sussexiana." was sold for $6; "Bibliotheca Americana Nova," with memoranda by Mr. Corwin, $11.50; a "Catalogue of the Library of Miss Curren, at Eshton Hall," with three autograph letters, only 40 copies printed, $5.25; a fine copy of "Pantographia" $5.50; "A Dissertation upon English Typographical Founders and Foundries," with an Appendix, very curious and scarce, $6.50; a copy of Bartlett's "Dictionary of Americanisms," $6.50; Horne Tooke's "Diversions of Purley," 2 vols. 4to., half calf, $5.25; a large paper uncut copy of the

"Opera Omnia" of Isocrates, 3 vols. 4to., Paris, Didot, 1782, only $12; Barlow's "Columbiad," 4to., best edition, with Smirke's Illustrations, $15; "Legendæ Catholicæ; a Lytle Boke of Seyntlie Gestes," of which only 40 copies were printed, $3.75; a copy of the first edition of Rogers' "Italy," 2 vols. 8vo., Turkey morocco, $9; "Witt's Recreations, Augmented with Ingenious Conceites for the Wittie, and Merrie Medicines for the Melancholie, with a Thousand Outlandish Proverbs," 2 vols. 12mo., published at £3 3s., $3.25. The collection was particularly rich in old almanacs. A volume containing 20 "Poor Richard's Almanacks," purchased by Mr. Corwin at the sale of the late E. D. Ingraham's library at Philadelphia, each leaf being mounted on laid paper, and the whole elegantly bound, was taken by Mr. Norton, for $62.50. At a sale some years since, which included eighteen copies of "Poor Richard," Mr. Corwin gave $12 each, $216, though, we believe, they were not intended for his own collection. The catalogue contained an unusually large list of works on Calligraphy and Stenography. A volume on Book-keeping entered in this division, entitled "The Maner and Fourme how to keep a perfecte reconyng, after the order of the moste worthie and notable accompte of Debitour and Creditour, etc., etc.," folio, black letter, Lond. 1553, sold for $3.25. "Finden's Royal Gallery of British Art," 48 line engravings, proofs before letter, published at £80, fetched $50. A Bible, supposed by Dibdin and others to be the second edition of the Latin Bible, printed at Strasburg ,by Eggesteyn, $20; a copy of Eliot's Indian Bible, 2 vols. 4to, was purchased by Norton for $200.

This Bible is printed in the Natick or Nipmuck language, remarkable for its long words. We believe this same copy was sold some years since by Bartlett & Welford for $40. A copy of the first edition of the Rhemish Testament, $20. The gem of the collection was Tyndal's "Translation of the Pentateuch, Emprinted at Marlborow in the land of Hesse, by me, Hans Luft, in the yere of our Lord, 1530, the XVII. days of Januarii," 18mo., black letter, with numerous curious wood cuts, a suberb copy in antique morocco, by Hayday, with fac similes by Harris. This volume cost over $100 to bind and complete, and is considered the second best copy known. On account of some delay in binding, this bibliographical treasure was not received in time for the sale; we understand that Mr. Norton offered $300 for it, but it was not accepted. An Illuminated Missal of the thirteenth century brought $12; "Commentary on the Penitential Psalms," black letter, Wynkyn de Worde, 1507, $30; "Institvtion of a Christen Man; conteynge the Exposytion or Interpretation of the commune Creed, of the seuen Sacramentes, of the X Commandmentes, and of the Pater Noster, and the Ave Maria, Justyfication and Purgatory," 4to., black letter, Lond. 1537; $16; "Summa de Articulus Fidei et Ecclesiæ Sacramentes," Thomas de Aquinas, printed with the types of the Catholicon of 1460, and exceedingly rare; is one of the purest specimens of early typography by Guttenburg, and esteemed the earliest specimen of printing held in this country, was sold for $20, very low.

In the department of Theology, Mr. Corwin's Library possessed many curious and rare Tracts, with quaint titles, such as "Echoes from the Sixth Trumpet reverberated by a review of neglected remembrances. Imprinted in the year Chronogramically expressed in this seasonable prayer;—LorD haVe MerCIe Vpon Vs," by George Wither, 1661. $5; "The Belgick Pismire stinging the Slothful Sleeper, and awakening the diligent to watch, fast and pray," &c., 1622, $2.25. "The Boke of the Olde God and the Newe, of the Old Fayth and the Newe, of the Old Doctryne and the Newe; or the Orygynale Begynnynge of Idolatrye," black letter, very rare, $3. "Fovr Godlye Sermons agaynst the Polvtion of Idolatrye," by John Calvin, 1561, $3.25. Davenport's "Discourse about Civil Government," $2.50. "The Rebuke Rebuked, in a brief answer to Caleb Pusey, his Scurrilous Pamphlet, entitled a Rebuke to Daniel Leeds, &c. Wherein *William Penn* his *Sandy Foundation* is fairly quoted, showing that he calls *Christ the Finite Impotent Creature*," N. Y., W. Bradford, 1703, $8; "Issachar's Asse Braying Vnder a double Burden; or, the Vniting of Churches, 1622, $4.50. "Christian Sodality, or the Catholic Hive of Bees," 1652, 50 cents. "The Connecticut Dissenter's Strong Box," 1802, $1. "The Dippers Dipped, or the Anabaptists ducked and plunged over head and ears at a disputation at Southwark," etc. By D. Featly, 1657, $7. Among the law books was a "Complete collection of the Laws of Maryland," Annapolis, 1727, the first book printed in Maryland, and very rare, which sold for $27.50. Of works on America, the catalogue had a very good collection; a copy of Mather's "Magnalia Christi" brought $50. "A Relation of the Troubles which

have hapnd in New England, by reason of the Indians there," by Increase Mather, Boston, 1677, $19.
A further account of the "Tryals of the New England
Witches," by the same, Lond. 1693, $6.50. "Historia
der Newen Welt, &c." Marburg and Frankfort, 1557,
$12. There were many volumes of rare pamphlets;
one set, 39 in number, chiefly political, relating to
Colonial difficulties, brought $195. Among Auto-
graphs, a book of about 300, none very rare, sold for
$37. An original letter of Fulton, referring to the
establishment of steamers on James River, $10; one
of Cotton Mather, dated Boston, 1712, sold for $21.

A number of orders for the above sale were received
from London Booksellers, and purchases to a consid-
erable extent were made for the British Museum.

MR. BRINLEY'S TREASURES SCATTERED.

(*March, 1879.*)

A TOTAL OF $48,830.75 FOR ABOUT 2,700 LOTS—INCI-
DENTS AND PRICES OF YESTERDAY'S SALE—
THE PRINCIPAL PURCHASERS—PROFITS
OF BOOK-COLLECTING.

The auctioneer's hammer fell upon the last volume
of the first part of Mr. Brinley's American library at
9:15 last evening, completing the dispersion of the
greatest collection of Americana ever sold in this
country, and which, in some departments, stood unrivaled in the world. There was no fag end to the
sale, the last day being quite as interesting as any that
preceded it, though the average of prices was natur-

ally lower, as many of the lots were unbound tracts and pamphlets of no special rarity. But the monotony of half-dollar bids was often relieved by an animated contest for a precious "nugget." Such, for instance, was the extremely rare copy of the Saybrook "Confession and Platform" of the Connecticut Churches, New-London, 1710, the first book printed in the State. This copy is nearly uncut, abounding in proof leaves, and Mr. Leiter, of Chicago, bid it off at $100. Another copy, slightly smaller, went to Yale for $75, and the Lenox Library secured the third copy at the same price. Another exceedingly rare book, Bernard Romans' "Annals of the Troubles in the Netherlands," two volumes in one, Hartford, 1778–82, fetched $41. An uncut copy of Ezra Stiles's "Three Judges of King Charles I.," Hartford, 1794, accompanied by another copy containing the plates, sold for $30. The scarce tracts relating to the Susquehanna Company's land sold for good prices, $61 being paid for "Gale's Letter to J. W.," 1769, and $32 for "The State of the Lands," etc., New York, 1770. The first volume of verse ever printed in Connecticut, Roger Walcott's "Poetical Meditations," New London, 1725, fetched $40, for the Lenox Library. Major John Talcott's manuscript account-book, 1674–88, including his accounts as Treasurer during the Indian wars, 1675–6, fetched $105, and was bought by Mr. Hoadley for the Connecticut State Library. Among its other curious entries is an item acknowledging the receipt of a seven-year old Indian girl to balance accounts, and a payment of 10 shillings to William Edwards, "for taking Henry Green

out of the Dungeon, being dead, cutting off his legs to
save his irons, and seeing to his burial." A volume
of Silas Deane's Manuscript Memorials to Congress,
1798–9, fetched $45. There was a waking up over
lot No. 2171, "New Haven's Settling in New England, and Some Laws for Government," printed in
London in 1656. The bidding was determined, and
when it stopped the book was knocked down to J.
Hammond Trumbull for $380. This excessively rare
volume was a few years ago in the possession of John
Russell Smith, the London bookseller, who priced it
in one of his catalogues at £18. As soon as Mr.
Brinley received a catalogue, he at once ordered the
book by cable, and got it. About that time Mr.
Henry Stevens, of Vermont, and elsewhere, landed on
the shores of his adopted Albion, after a short visit to
this country. He made all haste to Smith's bookstore, intent on the purchase of this very copy. He
was informed that it was sold. With a look of inex-
pressible sadness, not unmixed with hope, he offered
to give £50 for the book if Mr. Smith would cancel
the first bargain. The incorruptible Mr. Smith refused, and "New-Haven's Settling" came to Hartford. Previous to its arrival the copy in the Antiquarian Society Library at Worcester was regarded
as unique. But Mr. Brinley had no regard for that
word. He straightway procured another copy. Mr.
W. F. Poole, of Chicago. chanced to find one in Cin-
cinnati, with which its owner, whose mind was doubtless intent on pigs, consented to part for $5, and it
was made over to Mr. Brinley for that sum. This
copy sold last night for $310, for the Connecticut

State Library. Its title and portions of the first leaf have been restored in fac-simile by Burt. A probably unique pamphlet of 15 pages by Roger Sherman, with his autograph, entitled "A Caveat against Injustice, or an inquiry into the Evil Consequences of a Fluctuating Medium of Exchange," New York, 1752, fetched $100. Two volumes of the *Connecticut Gazette*, from April 12, 1755, to March 5, 1757, went to the Yale Library at $160. Mr. Brayton Ives secured the first book printed in New Haven, a book of Yale College laws, printed in 1755, for $26; the first book printed in Hartford, Thomas's "Explanation" of the Saybrook platform, 1765, cost him only $5. A series of 11 very rare almanacs, various years from 1753 to 1770, fetched $99. The Lenox Library bought a copy of the Acts and Laws of Rhode Island, Newport, by James Franklin, 1730, for $130, and a series of acts and laws from 1745 to 1752, for $60. The same buyer secured for $50 Rev. James Macsparran's "America Dissected," 1733. The first book printed in Rhode Island, "The Rhode Island Almanac for the Year 1728," printed in that year by J. Franklin, was bought for the Library of Congress for $35. Thomas supposed the first production of the Rhode Island press to have been issued in 1732. A rare broadside poem relating to Dartmouth College, "The Wilderness shall Blossom as the Rose," probably written by John Wheelock, son of Dr. Eleazar Wheelock, and printed about 1774, fetched $5 for the Library of Congress.

An extraordinary degree of interest was aroused over the lots relating to the New Hampshire grants

and the disputes between New York, the Vermonters, and New Hampshire. Mr. Brinley had had
these very rare pamphlets bound uniformly in full
dark-green crushed levant morocco, plain, and all were
beautiful specimens of Bedford's best work. There
was a contest over each lot, but a single buyer,
through an unlimited bid left with a local bookseller,
bore down all opposition, and secured them all at the
following prices: "Some Reflections on the Disputes,"
probably written by Col. John H. Lydius, and printed
in 1764, $28; "The Petition of the Grantees of New
Hampshire," with autograph signatures of 57 Grant-
ees, $26; "The Memorial of Peter Livius," 1773, $26;
Ethan Allen's "Brief Narrative," 1774, $45; the
same author's "Animadversory Address," 1778, $26;
"A Public Defense of the Right of the New Hampshire Grants," 1779, $100; Ethan Allen's "Vindica-
tion of the Vermonters," 1779, $105; Allen and Fay's
"Concise Refutation," 1780, $50; Bradley's "Ver-
mont's Appeal," $40; Allen's "Present State of the
Controversy," 1782, $49; a copy of "A Remonstrance
of the Court of the State of Vermont," 1783, $40.
Mr. L. E. Chittenden, coming in late, bought an uncut copy of "A Narrative of Ethan Allen's Captivity,"
by himself, 1779, for $22.50. After local history had
been pursued through the wilds of Vermont and New
Hampshire, and lost in the woods of Maine, there was
a brief return, in the addenda, to the time of the
Mathers. Robert Calaf's "More Wonders of the In-
visible World," a cropped, yet perfect copy, was sold
for $55; a copy disposed of earlier in the sale fetched
$190. The last lot sold contained Ethan Allen's

"Narrative," and other Vermont matter, and fetched $10.75.

The results of each day's sale are as follows:

Monday	$9,895 03	Thursday	$5,348 13
Tuesday	12,715 65	Friday	4,680 97
Wednesday	10,991 18	Saturday	5,199 79

Total $48,830 75

This is a good round sum for one-third of a private collection. Mr. Menzies's entire library fetched $50,000. The average per lot is $18.78 and a fraction. It is the general judgment of the best informed collectors who attended the sale, that the prices realized were high. There is no doubt that the estate of Mr. Brinley will receive, in the total sum, a handsome advance on the amount he expended on these books. It is getting to be understood that books are a safer investment than real estate. The results of the sale are important to bibliography, for the prices obtained will be quoted in hundreds of future catalogues, and they form, in bulk, a valuable report of the Americana market for the year 1879. Priced catalogues of the sale will soon command a good sum. Many private collections and public libraries have been greatly improved by purchase at this sale. The American Antiquarian Society's Library has filled many of the gaps that marred its collection of seventeenth century American books. The Lenox Library of this city has largely increased its stores of this class of books —the writings of the Mathers, witchcraft literature, etc. It is now measurably strong in these directions, in which, however, its owner has never aimed at com-

pleteness. The J. Carter Brown Library at Provi-
dence has been vastly strengthened in Mather books
through the liberal and judicious purchases of Mr. J.
R. Bartlett. The Library of Congress has expended
about $3,000 at the sale, and has secured a very desir-
able mass of literature from all departments of the
catalogue. Mr. Hoadley, of .the Connecticut State
Library, came down here with $5,000 to spend, of
which he has probably used not more than one-half,
reserving the other half for future opportunities. The
Yale representatives had a similar amount to use at
this sale, but it was not all spent. Dr. J. Hammond
Trumbull has bought about $5,000 worth of very de-
sirable lots for the Watkinson Library, of Hartford,
making usually very good bargains, for which he
seems to have a peculiar faculty, that is of great ser-
vice in the auction-room. He has also invested about
$1,500 for his own collection. Mr. Leiter, of Chicago,
has enriched his collection by innumerable purchases,
and the Chicago Public Library has greatly extended
its Americana. Mr. Murphy made several important
purchases for the Brooklyn Historical Society's
Library.

The scattering of such a collection of rare books
and the manner of their dispersion raise again the old
question, How long will these be any such books to
scatter? Two-thirds or more of the volumes that
Mr. Brinley has been thirty years in getting together
have gone into libraries whence they will never come
forth for sale. They are beyond the book-hunter's
reach. This phenomenon is ever repeating itself.
How long a time must elapse before the public libra-

ries will have absorbed all the books that are properly
called excessively rare? The process is slow, but it
is exceeding sure, and the ultimate consequence seems
to be as certainly demonstrable as a proposition in
geometry.

The Washington sale, December 12, 1890, at Thomas
Birch & Son's auction rooms, 1110 Chestnut street, was
continued yesterday. The sale was devoted principally
to books, many of which had autographs of either the
Washington or Lewis families. As was the rule at
the first night's session, high prices were given for
nearly everything bought, because, possibly, the articles were in such good company. The ladies who
were buying for the Ladies' Mt. Vernon Association
of the Union made many purchases, and bid so spirit-
edly that they became the observed of all. There
were many articles knocked down to a party giving
the name of Wilson, who happened to be Mr. Benjamin T. Cable, of New York.

Henry Horne's "Loose Hints," printed in Edin-
burgh, 1787, and bearing Washington's autograph on
the title page, was the first article on the catalogue.
It was knocked down to the Mount Vernon Association at $85. The same Society gave $77 for Her-
vey's "Meditations," London, 1750, which bears four
autographs of Mary Washington, the mother of the
first President, and made an interesting fight for a
volume of the "Female Spectator," of which there
were three. However, they were purchased by Mr.
Murphy, agent for W. R. Hearst, the California mil-
lionaire, for $160 a volume.

Martha Washington's Bible, which has had 300

copper plates engraved by John Sturt inserted, was
won, after a lively fight, by Mitchell, the New York
bookseller, for $760, and A. J. Bowden, the member
of the firm who made the purchase, remarked after
the sale that it was very cheap at that figure. The
book, which was printed at Oxford, 1789, and which
contains two signatures of Martha Washington, in
addition to the family record of the Lewises, was
started at $500. It ran up rapidly to $750, and then,
just as the auctioneer was about to drop the gavel,
$760 was bid, the highest amount given yesterday.

After the Bible was sold, Martha Washington's fan,
described in the catalogue as "a beautiful composition
of ivory, steel and lace," which is extremely small,
was the cause of much spirited bidding. From a
start at $50 it ran rapidly, by $5 and $10, up to
$230—when it was awarded to " Wilson."

Gray's Poems, London, 1768, on the title page of
which is written "John Randolph, Virginia, 1787,"
was given to Hearst for $130, while a school book,
Rigg's "New American Latin Grammar," published
in New York, 1788, which had been used by Washington's adopted son, and which had been enriched
with scribblings in a youthful hand of the original
owner, brought $12.

The "Grammatical Exercise Book," a copy book
in the handwriting of Eleanor Parke Custis, Washington's adopted daughter, was sold to W. R. Benjamin, of New York, for $20. A volume of piano
music once owned by that lady, which included,
among other rare pieces, the overture to "The De-
serter," "The Federal March," as performed in the

procession July 4, 1788, and the chorus sung before Washington as he passed under the triumphal arch raised on the Trenton bridge, April 21st, 1789, was knocked down to "Wilson" for $90. The same person got another music book, which contained the first edition of "Hail Columbia," for $70. Judge Mitchell was given another volume of music, which was considered valuable on account of a bust portrait of Washington engraved on the title page of the "Battle of Trenton," a sonata, for $115. The portrait is believed to be one of the rarest of Washington's, and Mr. Baker, the well-known collector, is said to have remarked that it was unknown to him.

Dr. Robert H. Lamborn, of New York, gave $20 for a common-looking oblong quarto, in boards, "Episcopalian Harmony," which bears the autograph of Eleanor Parke Lewis on the cover. The Doctor also became possessor of an invitation card of Washington, which "requested the pleasure of Miss Peggy Chew's company" at an entertainment, for $18. He also got a receipt signed by the General, for $15.

A portrait of Washington, which is supposed to have been painted by Gilbert Stuart, and which was bought at the sale of the effects of President Madison, went for $170. A letter signed by Washington at Valley Forge was sold for $150, although the letter was in another hand.

A small portrait, said to have been painted in Williamsburg, Va., in 1755, and supposed to represent George Washington at that time, was sold for $220, notwithstanding the fact that the auctioneer would not vouch for the truth of the statement, although he said he had every reason to believe it.

A finely painted portrait of Washington, supposed to have been the work of William Birch, went to Judge Mitchell for $90. The smallest price paid for anything at the afternoon session was 15 cents, given by the Mt. Vernon Association for three odd volumes of the "Penny Magazine."

The evening session concluded the sale, which settles the Washington estate, although other Washingtoniana are to be sold to-day. The Ladies' Mount Vernon Association of the Union made large purchases of books, which generally brought small prices as compared with the early part of the sale. Marshall's Life of Washington, 6 volumes, Philadelphia, 1804, went for $1.25 a volume. The second Boston Edition of the Official Letters of Washington, Boston, 1796, with the rare portrait by S. Hill, was knocked down to Judge Mitchell for $12.50. Two ledgers, containing accounts of various individuals with the executors of the Washington estate, were bought for $50 apiece. A large number of autograph letters from various eminent persons, in relation to the same estate, were sold at prices ranging from five cents to $5.50, the latter amount having been given for one by Henry Clay.

The most interesting incident in the evening's sale, and one which astonished the auctioneer himself, was the sale of the last lot. This was an innocent-looking lot of apparent rubbish, and was catalogued as "Documents and receipts received by the executors in settling the estate of George Washington." There were enough of them to fill a bushel basket, and some one started the lot with a bid of $7. He soon fell out of

the race, however, and only two were left in it.
These were W. R. Benjamin and A. J. Bowden, of
Mitchell's, New York. They fought for it by $10 at
a time, and it was finally knocked down to Mr. Benjamin. The lot was said to contain many interesting
and important documents, among them being a bill
for mourning worn at Washington's funeral.

The receipts for the day amounted to $4928, which
with those of the previous day, which were $9885 in-
stead of the amount published, makes a total of
$14,813.

Desiring to place as much bibliographical matter as
I have collected in this *brochure* for the edification of
old booksellers and collectors of old books, I extract
from an old copy of the *Public Ledger* of this city,
written—I forget when—at least a few years ago.
The data are interesting and the gossip good :

SOMETHING ABOUT OLD BOOKS AND THEIR BUYERS.

"Saur Bible, $275." This was the inscription
written on a piece of paper attached to an old leather-
covered book in the window of a Sansom street store
yesterday, and to a *Ledger* reporter, who entered the
store, Mr. Campbell, the proprietor, courteously
showed the curious volume. "It is a nice copy, isn't
it?" he queried, as he looked with an affectionate
sort of expression upon the work. It was "nice" in
a sense, and in that sense, doubtless, the very tattered

7

condition of the back and the general ancientry of the book's appearance had a great deal to do with its niceness.

"Isn't that a nice price, too?" he was asked. "The last one sold," was the reply, "was disposed of at the Brinley sale for $300. This one is, perhaps, the only original Saur Bible now offered for sale in this country, the others being in the hands of private collectors, who do not care to dispose of them. This, you will understand, is one of the original editions. The next edition is that worth only $15 a copy. This one was next to the Elliott Judson Bible, which was the first printed in America. The oldest Bible I have handled was the Coburger, published about 1488. I sold it to Dr. C. R. Early, a collector up in the State, for $30."

There were law books of all kinds and of nearly all sizes stacked about, and inquiries were made concerning them and their prices. "Old law books," said Mr. Campbell, "are extremely valuable when they are of the right sort. Some time ago I picked up a copy of the laws of New Jersey for $5. I knew the book, but nobody else at the sale seemed to have similar knowledge of it, as it was not specially designated. That book is worth $500. The first law book in the English language was the 'Doctor and the Student,' a conversational treatise on English laws, published about 1531. I sold a copy of it some time ago to a lawyer from Wyoming county for $30. Here is a specimen of what is known as the 'Second Bradford,' a copy of the laws of Pennsylvania, published in 1728. It is worth about $40. The next compilation after that is Benjamin Franklin's, about 1742; it is worth, say $15. The first Bradford edition, published in 1714, is worth $300 a copy. There does not exist in print a complete set of the Laws of Pennsylvania; there are only two complete sets that I know of at all. One set is owned by John Cadwalader, son of Judge Cadwalader, and the other is in the possession of F. C. Brightly. These sets are partially made up of certified copies."

To Mr. Stuart, who was found amid books that make a literary wilderness of his well-known store, the reporter observed: "You probably have some very rare old books here." "Well, yes," was the response, spoken with a hesitancy born of perplexing anticipations of having to name over some hundreds of works. "Do you find the demand of your customers running towards specialties?" was the next question. On this point it might be stated just here what Mr. Campbell said of specialists among old book hunters. "A gentleman was here on Saturday who wanted anything I could find in print on eating and drinking; another wants whatever I can get on fishing; a third has a weakness for books bearing on the French rebellion, and so on; there is scarcely a subject that doesn't have its patrons. "I have one customer," he said, "that wants whatever I can give him on the subject of Indians; another wants everything pertaining to the late war of the Rebellion." "The latter searcher is evidently a large buyer, then," remarked the reporter.

"The literature of the Rebellion is enormous," replied Mr. Stuart. "Here is Bartlett's Catalogue, pre-

pared in 1864–5, and it gives 6073 distinct titles of
works and papers on that subject. Since that time
there have been fully 20,000 more published. So you
can judge from that what a task it is to try and get a
library complete on that subject. The gentleman I
refer to takes matter from public documents and even
from magazine articles, and binds them separately, as
a contribution to his stock.

"Here is a somewhat rare old book [pointing to a
large bound volume laying on a desk] that I got hold
of a few days ago. This is the Ephrata Martyr
Book, published by the Dunkards at Ephrata, in this
State, in 1748. It is one of the handsomest specimens of colonial typography that I have ever seen,
and one of the largest ever published. I traced it
after no little trouble to the possession of a farmer
in Lancaster county, possibly a descendant of some
Dunkard family, and finally succeeded in getting it. It
is worth $100. The farmer brought it here himself.
When the Pennsylvania Historical Society bought
from Abraham H. Castle his collection of German
Colonial imprints, probably the largest in the State, he
put the whole lot of them in a big wagon, drove down
here with them from his home in Bucks county, and
delivered them to the Historical Society."

I have noted at various times the prices brought by
rare books at auctions and at private sales. "The
Mazarin Bible" is so called because it first was owned
by the celebrated Cardinal Mazarin, or at least it
was first noticed by bibliographers in the Cardinal's

library. There are but few copies extant, and when offered at sale they bring a large price. It bears *no date*, but the best authorities class it as printed about 1454. and 1456. There is no question but it is one of the earliest books printed. The largest price quoted at auction is $11,000. Elliot's Indian Bible is well known; the price has fluctuated very much, from $80 to $700. In Corwin's sale of books I find Field's Battle of Long Island brought $75. Harvand's Book, 2 vols., $100. Phillips' Historical Collection of Money, $28. This book was printed by Joel Munsell, of Albany, N. Y., in 2 vols., at $5. Life of Joseph Reed, by W. B. Reed, in 2 vols., cloth, $18. This book was published in this city by the old firm of Lindsay and Blakiston, and was very common thirty-five years ago. I have sold it for $150—it was published at $5. Stevens' Historical Nuggets, 2 vols., $25. A copy of my " Centennial Book of the Signers" brought at Murphy's sale, in New York in 1884, $445. It was the Large Folio Edition, and sold by me for $25. This copy was largely illustrated with *original autographs*—how many I don't know. In Cook's sale a similar copy, *not* illustrated, without additions, brought $25.

I published in the *Historical Magazine*, May 1859, a Memoir and Bibliography of William Bradford's works. He was among the earliest printers of books in this country, and being the *earliest American imprints*, his works are eagerly sought after by old book collectors. I mention elsewhere where one of his works, "The Laws of New York," brought at Brindley's sale $1600, though he had bought it in this city for $16.. I deem this account will be of value to the old booksellers and old book collectors.

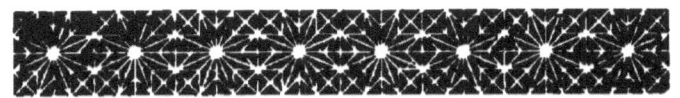

BIBLIOGRAPHY OF WILLIAM BRADFORD'S BOOKS.

CATALOGUE of works printed by William Bradford, A. D. 1686. In the Quaker Library in London is a small 4to. tract of four to six leaves, printed by Bradford, at Philadelphia, in 1686. I have not been able to procure the title. (This on the authority of II. Stevens, Esq., who informs me he has the full title.)

I am unacquainted with the subject matter of the above, and can give no information respecting them. You will notice that they are only tracts, not books, in the correct acceptation of the word.

A. D. 1687. An almanac for the year of the Christian account, 1687, particularly respecting the meridian and latitude of Burlington, but may indifferently serve all places adjacent, by Daniel Leeds, Student in Agriculture. Printed and sold by William Bradford, near Philadelphia, Pa., pro anno 1687.

This is a sheet almanack, with a compartment for each of the months, the year commencing with March and ending with February; at the bottom is an explanation, list of the eclipses for the year, courts and fairs at Burlington and Philadelphia, with some short rules in husbandry.

Some, if not all copies, have a notice that "There is now in the Press The excellent Privilege of Liberty and Prosperity, to which is added a Guide for the Grand and Petit Jury."

This has always been considered to be the first issue from Bradford's press, until the discovery of the tract in the Quakers' Library at London.

A. D. 1688. The Temple of Wisdom for the Little World in Two Parts. The First Philosophically Divine, treating of the Being of all Beings, and whence everything hath its original, as Heaven, Hell, Angels, Men and Devils, Earth, Stars, and Elements, and particularly of all mysteries concerning the Soul; and of Adam before and after the Fall. Also the Treatise of the four Complexions, with the Causes of Spiritual Sadness, etc. To which is added a postscript to all Students in Arts and Sciences, etc. The Second Part, Morally Divine, Contains:

First. Abuses, Stript and Whipt, by Geo. Wither, with a description of Fair Virtue.

Secondly. A Collection of Divine Poems from Fr. Quarles.

Lastly. Essays and Religious Meditation of Sir Francis Bacon, Knight.

Collected, Published and intended for general Good, by D. L. Printed and sold by Wm. Bradford, in Phila. Anno 1688.

Collation. Title, one leaf; Preface, two and a half pages. Jacob Baume, to the Doctors, etc., three pages, pp. 1 to 126. Title to second part with Bradford's imprint, 1688. Notice to the Reader, pp. 3 to 87, and one page of errata. Quarto.

Bacon's Works. Montague's Edition, vol. 16, note 31. (Life, page 37.) At the close of the note, Mr. Montague states that this was the first book printed in Philadelphia, and I have no doubt of it; my copy is in the finest state of preservation, and clean as when issued. 'Tis the rarest of rare American books.

A. D. 1689. Gershom Bulkeley. A tract by him, printed by Bradford at Philadelphia, in 1687; eight leaves 4to.; a copy of which is in the New York Historical Library, and another in the British Museum (same authority as above).

A. D. 1689. Keith's Presbyterian and Independent Visible Churches in New England. Printed by Bradford at Philadelphia, 1689. This work was reprinted at London in 1689–1691 A. D.

The People's Rights to Election, or Alteration of Government in Connecticut, argued in a letter by Gershom Bulkeley, Esq., one of their Majesties' Justices of the Peace in the County of Hartford, &c. 4to., Philadelphia, 1689.

A. D. 1692. Blood will Out; or an Example of Truth by Plain Evidence of the Holy Sriptures; viz., Pardon Tillinghast, B. Keech and Cotton Mather, and a few words of a letter to Cotton Mather. By George Keith, Philadelphia. Printed and sold by Wm. Bradford, 1690, 4to., pp. 74.

A. D. 1690. A Refutation of Three Opposers of Justice in the Tryal, Condemnation, Confession, and Execution of Thomas Sutherland, who barbarously murdered John Clark of Philadelphia, and was executed at Salem, in West Jersey, 23 February, 1692.

A. D. 1692. Keith's Serious Appeal, etc. Bradford, Philadelphia, 1692.

A. D. 1692. An Appeal from the Twenty-eight Judges to the Spirit of Truth and True Judgment in all Faithful Friends, called Quakers, that meet at this yearly meeting at Burlington, the 7th month, 1692. 4to., no date or place.

This book was printed at Philadelphia in 1692, by William Bradford, for which he was imprisoned upon the charge of "uttering and spreading a malicous and seditious paper." His tools and type were taken away from him, and this was the beginning of the persecution which afterward drove him with his printing from Philadelphia to New York in 1693. This excessively scarce little quarto consists of eight pages only.

A. D. 1692. A Serious Appeal to all the more Sober, Impartial, and Judicious people of New England, into whose hands this may come. Printed and sold by Wm. Bradford, at Philadelphia, in Pennsylvania, 1692. 4to., pp. 72.

A. D. 1692. A True Copy of Three Judgments given forth by a party of men called Quakers, at Phila., against George Keith and his friends; with two Answers to the said Judgments. 4to., sheets, good condition. Printed by Wm. Bradford, in Philadelphia, 1692.

On the verso of the last leaf of this very rare and curious book is a list of the Books to be sold by Wm. Bradford, in Philadelphia, 1692, with the prices; and at the bottom of the page is the following note: "And whereas it is reported that the printer, being a favourer of G. K., he will not print for another, which is the reason that the other party appear not in print as well as G. K., These are to signify that the printer hath not yet refused to print anything for either party; and also signifies that he doth not refuse, and is willing and ready to print anything for either party; and also signifies that he doth not refuse, and is willing and ready to print anything for the future that G. K.'s opposers shall bring to him." 15 pages, 4to.

A. D. 1692. A Counter Testimonial, Signed by

seventy-eight persons, disavowing all those concerned in the denial of Geo. Keith. Written by Geo. Keith, 1692. An Expostulation with Samuel Jennings, Thos. Lloyd, and the rest of the seventy-eight unjust judges and signers of the condemnation against Geo. Keith and his friends.

A. D. 1692.   The plea of Innocent, etc.

A. D. 1693.   Keith's Heresie, and Hatred, etc. Bradford, Philadelphia, 1693.

A. D. 1693.   New England's spirit of persecution, and transmitted to Pennsylvania, and the pretended Quaker found persecuting the true Christian Quaker, in the trial of Peter Boss, Geo. Keith, Thos. Budd, and Wm. Bradford, at the session held at Philadelphia, December, 1692, etc.   4to., printed 1693, where not mentioned, pp. 15.

This is Bradford's own account of his trial; it has been questioned whether this volume was really printed in Philadelphia, because Bradford having suffered imprisonment for printing and publishing "The Appeal," would not likely have ventured to issue a work of this character there, and thereby subject himself to a probable recurrence of difficulty. It has been surmised that the volume might have been printed in New York; but if that were the case, he could have had no possible motive for withholding his name from the title page.

The work was reprinted in London in the same year, and I find the title of the English ending as follows: Printed in Pennsylvania, "Reprinted in London, for R. Baldwin, 1693," which, in my opiniou, effectually dispels all doubts about the matter. In addition to which, Bradford having been discharged from prison and had his press restored to him by Governor Fletcher, on the sole ground of his having been imprisoned for a religious difference, could not have had any misgivings whatever respecting the publication of above recital of the circumstances attending his trial.

New York, A. D. 1692. A Proclamation, being a warning to the people to erect a beacon to be fired as a signal on the approach of the French fleet, then expecting as an invading force, and for all to hold themselves in readiness. Printed by W. Bradford, at New York, Printer to their Majesties, 1692. Supposed to be the first production of Bradford's press in New York. Nothing else is known to exist bear this date.

New York, A. D. 1693. A volume of the Laws of the Colony, &c. Printed and sold by Wm. Bradford, Printer to their Majesties, at the sign of the Bible, in New York, 1693.

New York, A. D. 1694. The Laws and Acts of General Assembly for their Majesties' Province of New York, as they were enacted in divers Sessions,

the first of which began April 24, A. D. 1691.
Printed at New York by Wm. Bradford, Printer to
their Majesties, King William and Mary; folio, no
cover, 1694.

This volume embraces all the laws up to date of
publication. The Acts of each session seem to have
been published separately.

New York, A. D. 1696. A Letter of Advice to a
Young Gentleman leaving the University, concerning
his Behavior and Conversation in the World. By R.
L., 24mo., pp. 45. Printed and sold by Wm. Brad-
ford, printer to his Majesty, King William, at the
Bible, in New York, 1696.

This rare little book is the earliest book known to
have been printed in the city of New York, with the
exception of the Laws of the Colony, which appeared
in 1694. Both were printed by the celebrated Wm.
Bradford. This volume may be considered unique;
it is the only one that I have seen or heard of. It
was sold at the sale of the late Mr. E. B. Corwin's
library, for $12.50. The author was doubtless Rich-
ard Lyon, for an account of whom see Allen's Bio-
graphical Dictionary.

New York, A. D. 1696. A Reprint of a London
Gazette, containing an account of an engagement with
the French. The first newspaper printed in America.

New York, A. D. 1698. The Proceedings of His Excellency, Earl Bellemont, Governor of New York, and his Council, on the 8th of May, 1692. Printed and sold by Wm. Bradford, Printer to the King, New York, 1698, one sheet folio.

New York, A. D. 1699. A Trumpet sounded out of the Wilderness of America, which may prove as a warning to the Government and People of New England, to beware of Quakerism, wherein is shown how, in Pennsylvania and thereway, where they have the government in their own hands, they hire and encourage men to fight, and how they prosecute, fine, and imprison, and take away goods for conscience sake; by Daniel Leeds. Printed by Wm. Bradford, Printer to the King, New York, 1699.

New York, A. D. 1702. A refutation of a dangerous and hateful opinion maintained by Mr. S. Willard, an independent Minister of Boston, and President at the Commencement at Cambridge, in New England, July 1st, 1702, 4to. No title, pp. 7.

New York, A. D. 1702. An account of the illegal trial of Nicholas Bayard. Printed by William Bradford, at the sign of the Bible in New York, 1702.

New York, A. D. 1703. A Reply to Mr. Increase Mather's Printed Remarks on a Sermon Preached by G. K., at her Majesty's Chapel in Boston, the 14th of June, 1702. In vindication of the six Good Rules in

Divinity there delivered. Which he hath attempted (though very Feebly and Unsuccessfully) to refute, by Geo. Keith, M. A. Printed and sold by William Bradford, at the Bible in New York. 1703, 4to., pp. 35.

New York, A. D. 1703. The Rebuker Rebuked, in a Brief Answer to Caleb Pusey his Scurrilous Pamphlet, Entitled, A Rebuke to Daniel Leeds, etc. Wherein Wm. Penn, his Sandy Foundation is fairly quoted, showing that he calls Christ The Finite Impotent Creature, by Daniel Leeds. Printed and sold by Wm. Bradford at the Bible in New York, 1703. 4to. Title, To the Reader, one leaf, pp. 5 to 11.

New York, A. D. 1703. The spirit of Railing Shimel, and of Baal's four hundred Lying Prophets entered into Caleb Pusey, and his Quaker Brethren in Pennsylvania, who approve him. 4to., printed and sold by Wm. Bradford, at the sign of the Bible in New York.

New York, A. D. 1703. A Sermon Preached at Kingstown, in Jamaica, upon the 7th of June. Being the Anniversary Fast of that Dreadful Earthquake which happened there in the year 1692, by William Corbin, T. B. Printed and sold by Wm. Bradford, at the Bible in New York, 1703. 4to., Epistle, 1 leaf and 16 pp.

New York, A. D. 1704. Some brief remarks upon a late book, entitled "George Keith once more brought to the Test," etc., having the name of Caleb Pusey at the end of the preface, and C. P. at the end of the book (W. Bradford, New York, 1704). 4to., pp. 20.

This volume has no title page, and was doubtless published without one. It was written by George Keith, and is dated March 2d, 1704, over his signature. A great portion of the matter relates to Bradford's trial and his final discharge, with the restoration of his printing implements by Governor Fletcher.

New York, A. D. 1704. An answer to Mr. Samuel Willard (one of the Ministers at Boston in New England). His reply to My Printed Sheet, called A Dangerous and Hateful Opinion maintained by him, viz: That the Fall of Adam and all the sins of men, necessarily came to pass by virtue of God's Decree, and his determining both of the will of Adam and all other men to sin, by George Keith, M. A. Printed and sold by Wm. Bradford, at the sign of the Bible in New York, 1704. Dedicated to his Excellency Edward Viscount Cornbury, Captain General, and Governor-in-Chief, etc., etc. 4to., pp. 41.

New York, A. D. 1704. The notes of the True Church. with the Application of them to the Church of England, and the Great Sin of Separation from Her. Delivered in a Sermon, preached at Trinity Church, New York, before the Administration of the Holy

5

Sacrament, at the Lord's Supper, 7th of November, 1703, by Geo. Keith, M. A. Printed and sold by Wm. Bradford, at the sign of the Bible in New York, 1704. 4to., Title, Epistle, 3 leaves, pp. 20.

New York, A. D. 1705. The Great Mystery of Foncroft Discovered, and the Quaker plainness and Sincerity Demonstrated. First to their Great Apostle, Geo. Fox. Secondly, In their late Subscribing the Oath or Act of Abjuration. Introduced with two letters written by George Fox to Coll. Lewis Morris, deceased, exactly spelled and Printed as in the Originals, which are now to be seen in the Library at Burlington, in New Jersey, and will be proved (by the likeness of the Hand, &c.) to be the Handwriting of the Quakers' learned Fox, if desired. To which is added, A Postscript into some remarks on the Quaker's Almanack for this year 1705. 4to., pp. 16.

New York, A. D. 1706. John Sharpe. A Sermon—preached at Trinity Church in New York, Aug. 13, 1706, at the funeral of Katherine Lady Cornbury, heiress to the Duke of Richmond and Lenox, and wife of Lord Cornbury, Governor of New York, New Jersey. 4to. Printed and sold by Wm. Bradford at the Bible in New York.

New York, A. D. 1709. An Alarm Sounded to Prepare the Inhabitants of the World to Meet the Lord in the Way of his Judgment, by Bath Bowers.

Dated at the end Philadelphia, July 1709, but evidently printed by Bradford at New York. 4to., pp. 23.

New York, A. D. 1710. Lex Parliamentaria, etc.

New York, A. D. 1710. Acts of the General Assembly of New York, now in force. Bradford's usual imprint.

New York, A. D. 1717. The Laws and Acts of the General Assembly of his Majesty's Province of Nova Cæsarea or New Jersey, as they were enacted by the Governor, Council, and General Assembly, for the time being, in divers sessions. The first of which began in November, 1703. Printed and sold by John Bradford, Printer to the King's most excellent Majesty for the province of New Jersey, 1717.

OLD BOOK COLLECTORS.

HAVE given in the earlier portion of these memoirs some statements about the *earliest* old book collectors I have met: here I shall close by sketching the *very few* we have to-day.

The true bibliomaniac, I am sorry again to have to repeat, is a rarissimo—nearly as scarce as the dodo. We have a few that collect books and have fine libraries; but the true Dibdin man—the man that cannot pass an old book store, or even an old junk shop; that will travel miles to enrich his collection; that has not time even to dress decently; that lives in his library, sleeps in it, surrounded by folios, quartos, in fact, every size; that eats his meals there; that smokes his pipe; whose atmosphere smells musty, and cleanliness is almost a vice—this class of men are rare. I do not say all these peculiarities are even necessary or desirable, but such men do live, have lived, and no doubt will always live.

I know one man in this city, the honorable Judge Pennypacker, who possesses the true spirit of a bibliomaniac. His specialty is early American imprints

and nearly all Pennsylvania early imprints. It is a
pleasure to meet him. He is suave, affable and kind
to all, and extremely liberal in his dealings. His
library consists of over 3000 early imprints: the Ephrata imprints number 100; Franklin's imprints, 150;
Sauer's imprints, 160; he has the *first printed* Broad-
side of Sauer; Pennsylvania Almanacks of the last
century, 200; Poor Richard's Almanac, 30; early
maps of Pennsylvania; he has the earliest of German-
town (1686) Pastorius Gradation, printed about 1676.
His collection of books of David Rittenhouse is the
most perfect known.'

The most perfect and numerous collection of Chris-
topher Sowers is in the possession of William Sowers,
late publisher. I have sold to him over forty years
ago, when such books were not in demand, a large
number. I have sold Sower's Bibles, and fine copies
too, from $2 to $4; now they bring, as in Brindley's
sale, over $300—this was an exceptionally fine copy.
A poor copy was sold at auction in this city a few
weeks ago and only brought $4, but a good copy will
bring $25.

Howard Edwards, to whom I sold books forty
years ago, has made a specialty of collecting old Bibles,
and early printed Episcopal Prayer Books. He is
one of those collectors of books that if he had the
wealth of a Gould would be princely in his purchases.

His scanty purse has enabled him, with exemplary economy, to have the largest collection of old Bibles and Episcopal Prayer Books in this city.

Charles Mann has been collecting dramatic works for over thirty years, and has the largest dramatic library in this city.

Mr. Noble has a noble heart. He is a poor artisan, works for his daily bread, but would rather buy a rare, good book than a suit of clothes. His specialty is books on Free Thought, and he probably has the best collection of this class in this city. He also collects books on America and the late war, and he buys with judgment and extensive knowledge of books.

The McAlisters, W. A. and John, still love books, a taste they inherited from their much respected father, who was a genuine collector.

C. P. Bement, a rich man, I am glad to hear has become a good purchaser of books and also patronizes the fine arts.

W. S. Baker, the Washington authority, has linked his name among the Washingtonian authorities of the day and in such a manner as to reflect credit on himself and has obtained a niche in history. His literary works were not written for money, but for the love of his Fatherland. He is a kind and affable man, and generous in his purchases.

F. J. Dreer's specialty is autographs, and the very

fine collection of autographs which he has been collecting for over forty years; he has generously given them to the Historical Society of this city. He has a fair library of books, and in his lifetime has bought generously.

C. R. Hildebran, librarian to the Athenæum Library, has devoted himself to the study of old books, and has published a work on Pennsylvania literature—a transcript of all the early titles of the books published in this State, which an untiring industry could collect from all the old newspapers printed in this State. Great credit is due to him for indefatigable industry.

Simon Gratz has a fine library, and still collects old books; but his specialty is collecting autographs, and it is said that he has the largest collection in America. I have sold him many, but have not seen his collection as a whole.

R. C. Davis, who died two years ago, was a generous and noble man. He had a fine collection of books and coins, but his autographs were his pride. His collections of coins and autographs were among the finest in the country. After his death they were sold intact.

W. H. Kemble is a book collector, and it said he has quite a library on the " Letters of Junius."

E. Leslie Gilliams is a young journalist, and I am

glad to see he is moping about old-book stores, and is devoted to the collection of local history, and soon will have a fine collection. I trust he will ardently continue his pursuit, and time will reward his labors with joy.

Clarence Clark, a wealthy gentleman of this city, I learn, some years ago collected a very fine library, and is still collecting books—published a very fine catalogue of his library. I have not seen it, but this is very encouraging, and shows that the old bibliographic spirit still lives, and the fashionable clubs do not grasp all.

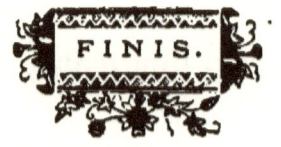
FINIS.

INDEX.

www.ingramcontent.com/pod-product-compliance
Lightning Source LLC
Chambersburg PA
CBHW032016010726
47493CB00007B/2430